● ● ● ● ● ●

She paused to try to get her breathing under control. There was nothing she could do about her tears.

"*Granny was 82 years old*," she bawled. "I knew that one day I would be standing here, speaking at her funeral, but she was so strong. I didn't think it would be no time soon. I sh – I shouldn't be standing here today. *What that man did to my granny ain't right.* He didn't have no right to do her like that – none of them people. Everyone in that store was *innocent*."

Her grimace was gut-wrenching. She felt the pastor's hand on her shoulder again.

"It's alright," the man told her. "That's alright..."

Zahra's breaths were audible. She squeezed her eyes closed. The tears streamed down her cheeks.

She told the crowd, "I will never understand how somebody can hurt somebody who never did anything to them. I don't understand why so many people in this country hate us. After all y'all did to us, all these years. All we ever did was *be born.* How can y'all hate us for that?"

Zahra sensed she was getting away from the purpose of the eulogy, but since her grandmother's death, she had quickly progressed through two stages of grief (denial and bargaining). She wasn't aware that she had transitioned to anger until that very moment.

"I'm sick of everybody on TV offering their thoughts and prayers," she announced gruffly. The bitterness in her heart strengthened her voice, if not her resolve. "This ain't the first time some white man opened fire on us, like we targets at the gun range. My granny deserves more than your *thoughts and prayers*. Somebody needs to do something about this. If y'all care about us, like y'all keep saying y'all do, then y'all need to do something to make them stop killing us! *I'm sick of it!*"

She was so angry, her whole body was trembling. She realized the pastor's hand was not just resting on her shoulder now. He was tenderly pulling her away from the mic.

● ● ● ● ● ●

1

TAKE ONE OF MINE

TAKE ONE
OF MINE

KEITH THOMAS WALKER

KEITHWALKERBOOKS, INC
This is a UMS production

KEITHWALKERBOOKS

Publishing Company
KeithWalkerBooks, Inc.
P.O. Box 690
Allen, TX 75013

For information write
KeithWalkerBooks, Inc.
P.O. Box 690
Allen, TX 75013

Copyright © 2022 Keith Thomas Walker

ISBN-13 DIGIT: 978-1-7356151-3-4
ISBN-10 DIGIT: 1-7356151-3-7
Library of Congress Control Number: 2022916432
Manufactured in the United States of America

Visit us at www.keithwalkerbooks.com

This book is dedicated to the memory of our martyrs. Unfortunately, there are too many to name. Most of them lost their lives before the days of hashtags.

MORE BOOKS BY KEITH THOMAS WALKER

Fixin' Tyrone
How to Kill Your Husband
A Good Dude
Riding the Corporate Ladder
The Finley Sisters' Oath of Romance
Blow by Blow
Jewell and the Dapper Dan
Harlot
Plan C (And More KWB Shorts)
Dripping Chocolate
The Realest Ever
Jackson Memorial
Sleeping With the Strangler
Life After
Blood for Isaiah
Brick House
Brick House 2
One on One
Brick House 3
Jackson Memorial 2
Backslide
Threesome
Backslide 2
Threesome 2
Election Day
Evan's Heart
Asha and Boom Part 1
Asha and Boom Part 2
Asha and Boom Part 3
Blurred Lines

NOVELLAS

Might be Bi Part One
Harder
Primal Part One
The Realest Christmas Ever
Hotline Fling

POETRY COLLECTION

Poor Righteous Poet

FINLEY HIGH SERIES

Prom Night at Finley High
Fast Girls at Finley High
Bullies at Finley High

Visit www.keithwalkerbooks.com for information about these and upcoming titles from KeithWalkerBooks

ACKNOWLEDGMENTS

Of course I would like to thank God, first and foremost, for giving me the creativity and drive to pursue my dreams and the understanding that I am nothing without Him. I would like to thank my beautiful wife and my mother for always pushing me to be the best I can be. I would like to thank Janae Hafford for being the best advisor, supporter and little sister a brother could ever have.

I would also like to thank (in no particular order) Beulah Neveu, Deloris Harper, Denise Fizer, Michele Halsey Hallahan, Priscilla C. Johnson, Edwina Putney, Melissa Carter, Cathy Atchison, Lanita Irvin, Cynthia Antoinette Taylor, Jason Owens, Ramona Brown, Johnathan Royal, Sharon Blount, BRAB Book Club, and Uncle Steven Thomas, one love. I'd like to thank everyone who purchased and enjoyed one of my books. Everything I do has always been to please you. I know there are folks who mean the world to me that I'm failing to mention. I apologize ahead of time. Rest assured I'm grateful for everything you've done for me!

CHAPTER ONE
HOPES AND PRAYERS

"So, what do you think their problem is? The ones that hate us, why do you think they feel that way?"

Zahra wasn't sure what to make of the question or the man asking it. They sat at a high-top table in a Starbucks on the west side of town. Outside, the mid-morning sun was blazing. The temperature inside was cool. Her companion was named David, but he'd told her he preferred to be called *Demon*. The moniker didn't seem to fit him, as he didn't appear to be evil or sinister. He was handsome, in an unassuming way. His skin was dark. He wore his hair in a box-style haircut. Zahra was twenty-three, and she guessed he was around her age. Demon wasn't muscular, but he wasn't skinny either.

She couldn't take her eyes off his.

He stared at her intensely, waiting for a response. She felt as if he could read her mind, which wouldn't have been helpful, because she didn't have a profound response to his question. The answer seemed obvious.

She asked him, "What do you mean? They hate us 'cause we black."

Zahra's skin tone was a couple of shades lighter than his. She wore her hair in long braids. She hadn't found much reason to smile in the past couple of months, and she wasn't smiling now. Without makeup, Demon would consider her features more serious than attractive, but he thought she was naturally beautiful, even in the midst of her despair.

"The ones who hate us do hate us just 'cause we black," he agreed. "But why is that? What makes a white man racist against a black man?"

She shrugged, still not sure where he was going with this. "They been hating us since slavery. They think they're better than us. They didn't see us as real people back then, and some of them still don't. The hate gets passed down from one generation to the next."

Demon nodded, studying her. "Do you think there's anything we're doing – *currently* – to contribute to the way they feel about us?"

She frowned. "*No*. All we're doing is existing."

He grinned at that. He was always so serious, she didn't think she'd ever seen his lips curve like that. He placed his forearms on the tabletop and leaned closer. Beyond the strong smell of coffee that permeated the café, she caught a whiff of his scent. It was faint. Not cologne, maybe deodorant. She thought his smell was pleasant.

"Well, let me ask you this," he said. "Do you think if our ancestors had rose from slavery and made something of themselves, and all of the black people in America today were homeowners, upper class – do you think they would still see us as inferior?"

10

She wasn't sure why his questions felt loaded, or why they were even having this conversation. She shrugged. "I don't know."

"Do you know why the slaves didn't hit the ground running and set up the next generation for success?" he asked. "Why is it that only 43% of blacks in this country own their home, compared to 72% for whites?"

She bristled. "They wouldn't let us. They stopped us from being successful."

"If you're talking about what this country did to us in the 1900's, you're right. They kept their foot on our neck that whole century. But the plan to hold us down started right after they freed the slaves. Every freed family was supposed to get forty acres of land. This land was supposed to be confiscated from the Confederates. The army offered to toss in some mules. This order was issued by Union General William T. Sherman in 1865. Do you know why it never came to be?"

Zahra shook her head. Demon was clearly more knowledgeable on this topic, and she was intrigued by the history lesson.

"Lincoln got popped," he said, "and his successor, Andrew Johnson, overturned the order. Most slaves started their free lives with nothing. A hundred and fifty years later, a lot of their descendants are still passing down *nothing* to their kids. That was definitely the case for my family. My father was poor. His father was poor. His father was too..."

Zahra held his gaze for a few beats and then looked around. There were white people in the coffee shop with them. Demon didn't seem concerned about having this conversation in their presence.

11

"How do you think we can fix it?" he asked. "If we're still being smothered by the horror of slavery and another hundred years of oppression, how do we rise above it, so maybe the whites who choose to hate us won't be able to use our circumstances as an excuse?"

"I don't know." She watched his eyes again. "Reparations?"

He grinned again, but it was humorless. "That was a trick question. What you need to understand is they don't need an excuse to hate us, and they will always have an excuse. They say they hate us because we're poor. They hate us because we're uneducated. They hate us if we go to college and make something of ourselves, because we're taking jobs away from more deserving white folks. They hate us if we abort our babies. They hate us if we have a lot of children. They hate us because we keep voting for Democrats. They hate us because we wanna take down the statues of our oppressors.

"The only bright spot in any of this is the whites who hate us are in the minority, and there's an even smaller number of them who are willing to act out violently. But I'm sure you know that a small number can do *massive* damage. It only took one man and one bullet to silence Martin Luther King."

Zahra's nostrils flared as they, along with her eyes, filled with moisture.

"Then there's nothing we can do about it," she asked, "just keep letting them attack us?"

After all the buildup, she felt Demon had led her to a demoralizing conclusion.

But he shook his head. "I didn't say there was nothing we could do about it, Zahra. I never said that..."

∞ ∞ ∞ ∞ ∞ ∞ ∞

Two months before meeting the mysterious intellectual at Starbucks, Zahra enjoyed what most would consider a *normal* life. School had never been something she was good at, so when she graduated from high school five years ago avoiding college was a no-brainer. After bouncing around a few menial jobs for the next four years, it was her grandmother who encouraged her to rethink that stance.

"Zahra," she had told her, "I know you and them books don't get along, but I saw a commercial on TV the other day talking about becoming a pharmacy tech in only a year. You remember you worked at Walgreens for a little bit when you first graduated. You didn't never think about going to school for that?"

Zahra had considered it at the time. The store she worked for made the training sound quick and easy. The only problem was she'd *just* graduated, and her position on more learning was resolute. But things were different when her grandmother broached the topic. Zahra wouldn't say the real world had been kicking her ass since she got her high school diploma, but she'd be lying if she said she'd been winning the rat race.

"I thought about it," she told her granny.

"Well, why you ain't did it then?" Granny wanted to know.

Zahra could do nothing but laugh at that. There was something about old age that made everything cut and dry. Then again, her grandmother had been of this mindset for as long as Zahra could remember.

"What's the number?" she asked her. "I know you wrote it down."

"Actually, I got it right here on my phone..."

Granny pulled a new iPhone from her purse that was still more of a mystery than a convenience. She found the number.

A year later, Zahra was a certified pharmacy technician. Less than a month after that, she landed her first job – at CVS, rather than Walgreens. Two weeks later, Zahra was hard at work on a Wednesday afternoon when her estranged mother called with news that shouldn't have been as surprising as it was.

"Mama dead."

Zahra stood stunned in the brightly lit pharmacy. All of the air had suddenly been sucked out of the room. "Wha, what are you talking about? I just saw Granny this morning, before I left for work."

"I know," her mother said. "It just happened."

Zahra could hear the emotion in her mother's voice then. She also heard a commotion in the background. Different voices. Frantic. Some screaming. Some angry.

Tears welled in Zahra's eyes. Her grandmother had raised her since she was six years old, back when her biological mother found an affection for crack cocaine.

"How – how did she die?"

The question came from a deep pit of despair. Even as she asked, Zahra understood that her mother's response would be unenlightening. Her grandmother was eighty-two years old. She was in relatively good health, but at that age, there was nothing wrong with Jesus simply calling you home. The life expectancy for black women in America was 78. Granny was blessed to have made it past that.

But her mother's response *was* enlightening, even though it made absolutely no sense.

"She got shot."

Zahra's tear-filled eyes widened. *"What?"*

She took a stumbling step backwards. Realizing she was falling, she reached blindly with her freehand and encountered a table that would support her. Half a dozen bagged and neatly stacked bottles of medication fell to the floor. She didn't notice her colleagues look in her direction. Another pharmacy tech whom she'd befriended rushed to her side.

Her mother was talking.

Zahra couldn't hear her. A loud hum was stuck somewhere between her ears.

"What?" she cried. *"I can't hear you, Mama."*

"... shot a lot of people," her mother was saying. "It was a white man. He shot a bunch of black people. He killed Mama. It's on the news, baby. *The man killed my mama...*"

∞ ∞ ∞ ∞ ∞ ∞ ∞

The next two hours were worse than any nightmare Zahra's subconscious could've conjured. Her brother picked her up from work and drove her to the only place she'd ever called home. There were so many cars parked in front of her grandmother's house, her brother had to drop her off while he went to find an available parking spot down the street. Inside the home, Zahra was greeted by faces she recognized, some she loved, some she and her grandmother had despised. All were grief stricken. All confused. Most were in the living room. That was where Zahra found her mother.

Her mother rushed to her and held her tightly.

15

"Baby, this is so bad," she cried against the side of Zahra's head. *"This so bad."*

Although Zahra needed to be comforted, needed to feel that her family was there for her, and they would get through this, she stiffened in her mother's embrace and then pushed her away. It was hard to breathe. In a trance-like state, she continued moving through the crowd. Uncle Jimmy, Aunt Gladys, Aunt Yolanda, everyone was there. Most were watching Granny's TV, sitting on Granny's couch. Zahra wanted to tell them that Granny didn't like to have this many people in her house – she didn't want to clean up after so many folks – but Zahra couldn't find her voice.

Every part of her body felt like it was losing the ability to function.

She felt like she was dying from some unknown, debilitating illness as she stood shoulder to shoulder with her cousins and stared at the television. A reporter stood outside of a supermarket. Zahra recognized it as the neighborhood Walmart, the only place to get fresh fruit and vegetables for fifteen miles in either direction. Granny drove there once a week to restock their refrigerator and pantry. Whenever Zahra wasn't working, she would go with her. She had fond memories of pushing the cart around the big store with her granny.

On the television, the store looked the same, but nothing about it was normal. Too many police and ambulances. Zahra wondered if her grandmother was still inside. The thought of her grandmother lying amidst what had to be complete carnage caused her to wail and lose her balance again.

She felt strong hands on her.

She didn't remember much about the rest of that day.

∞ ∞ ∞ ∞ ∞ ∞ ∞

By day two, the killer had been identified: Twenty-two-year-old white man named Brandon Guillory.

His motive was also revealed: He subscribed to *The Great Replacement* theory. Brandon believed blacks and other minorities were pursuing a calculated agenda to replace the white man, who was the rightful owner of the United States.

Brandon lived in Plano, a predominately white city in northern Texas. On the day of the shooting, he traveled fifty miles to a mostly black neighborhood in Overbrook Meadows. According to information collected from message boards he frequented on the internet, he chose the Walmart because he knew he would "find a lot of black people there."

His weapon of choice was an AR-15 style rife and a Glock 19.

His death toll was 18 black souls, ranging in age from 18 to 82.

Fifteen additional shoppers experienced life threatening or life altering injuries.

The shooter remained on the scene for forty agonizing minutes, slowly marching down the aisles, shooting those who remained in the store who were injured but not yet dead. He doubled-back and shot his deceased victims again, just to be sure.

In the days that followed, Zahra refused to allow anyone to tell her how many times her grandmother had been shot or what part of her body had taken damage. All she knew was that her grandmother had to have a closed-casket funeral, and that was enough.

That alone was too much to know.

∞ ∞ ∞ ∞ ∞ ∞ ∞

Zahra was not an activist. She was nothing like Reverend Al Sharpton, who traveled to Overbrook Meadows to console and pray with the bereaved families and attend every one of their loved one's funerals. Zahra would never be a civil rights icon like Reverend Jesse Jackson, who once stood on the balcony of the infamous Lorraine Hotel and witnessed the assassination of Dr. Martin Luther King Jr. Jackson arrived in Overbrook Meadows along with throngs of reporters, politicians, well-wishers and looky loo's. On the day of her grandmother's funeral, Zahra met with both Jackson and Sharpton. She remembered that they held her hands and spoke to her at length. But to this day, she couldn't recall what either of them had told her.

She did not want to speak at her granny's funeral.

But despite the enormous amount of love her grandmother had put out into the world and the many people who loved her back, there was no doubt that Zahra was her closest relative. They had lived together, just the two of them, for the past seventeen years. As her grandmother's age began to catch up with her, Zahra had been the one to help her out of bed when her knees became stiff overnight. Zahra made her coffee and toast each morning; this was all the old woman would eat for breakfast. Zahra was the first face Granny saw each morning and the last person she spoke to each night.

Zahra tried to plan the words she would speak during her grandmother's eulogy. She'd even gone as far as jotting down a few notes as a memo in her phone. But as she stood

18

behind the podium at Ebeneezer Baptist Church, staring out at a crowd that was so dense, half of the attendees did not have a seat, none of the things she wanted to say seemed to matter.

Her eyes once again filled with tears as she stared down at her grandmother's coffin. She wasn't sure how long she stood there, saying nothing at all, until one of the pastors standing beside her touched her shoulder and said, "That's alright. Take your time."

Zahra looked up at the crowd then. She swallowed roughly. She took a deep breath, which came out in shudders. She spoke from the heart.

"Granny, my grandmama, she was the sweetest person I've ever known." The grief in her voice was palpable. She vaguely heard dozens of voices in the crowd echo their agreement. "She always gave whatever she could to help people," Zahra continued. "She gave *more* than she had. She never asked for anything in return."

She paused to try to get her breathing under control. There was nothing she could do about her tears.

"*Granny was 82 years old*," she bawled. "I knew that one day I would be standing here, speaking at her funeral, but she was so strong. I didn't think it would be no time soon. I sh – I shouldn't be standing here today. *What that man did to my granny ain't right.* He didn't have no right to do her like that – none of them people. Everyone in that store was *innocent*."

Her grimace was gut-wrenching. She felt the pastor's hand on her shoulder again.

"It's alright," the man told her. "That's alright..."

Zahra's breaths were audible. She squeezed her eyes closed. The tears streamed down her cheeks.

19

She told the crowd, "I will never understand how somebody can hurt somebody who never did anything to them. I don't understand why so many people in this country hate us. After all y'all did to us, all these years. All we ever did was *be born*. How can y'all hate us for that?"

Zahra sensed she was getting away from the purpose of the eulogy, but since her grandmother's death, she had quickly progressed through two stages of grief (denial and bargaining). She wasn't aware that she had transitioned to anger until that very moment.

"I'm sick of everybody on TV offering their thoughts and prayers," she announced gruffly. The bitterness in her heart strengthened her voice, if not her resolve. "This ain't the first time some white man opened fire on us, like we targets at the gun range. My granny deserves more than your *thoughts and prayers*. Somebody needs to do something about this. If y'all care about us, like y'all keep saying y'all do, then y'all need to do something to make them stop killing us! *I'm sick of it!*"

She was so angry, her whole body was trembling. She realized the pastor's hand was not just resting on her shoulder now. He was tenderly pulling her away from the mic.

"It's alright," he repeated. "That, that's alright."

Zahra looked down at her grandmother's casket one more time and backed away from the microphone on her own accord. She had nothing left to say – not to these people. She could give her grandmother a better eulogy tonight when she said her prayers, and the Lord was the only one listening.

CHAPTER TWO
ALL BAD

Zahra wasn't sure what to expect when she returned to her seat on the first row of the church. A sea of eyes were on her as she made what felt like a walk of shame past her grandmother's coffin. The eyes revealed mixed emotions. No one said anything to her after the service, when the immediate family was ushered to three awaiting limousines outside the church. But once they were inside the car, the occupants were able to speak freely. Zahra looked around and saw that she was sharing the vehicle with her mother, her uncle Jimmy, Aunt Cheryl and her great Aunt Agatha. Everyone was dressed in their finest dark colors. They all shared a resemblance, even if only slightly. Aunt Cheryl was the first to speak up.

Shaking her head she said, "Zahra, I know you hurting, but I don't think it was right for you to say what you said up there."

Her mother quickly jumped to her defense. "Leave her alone. You know what she's going through."

Ever since Sandra got clean, Zahra thought she tried to overcompensate for basically abandoning her youngest child at a time when Zahra needed her mother the most.

"I know what she's going through," Cheryl said. "I just said that. I know how much you're hurting," she repeated to Zahra. "But that doesn't make it okay to speak that way at your grandmother's funeral. There's a time and a place for everything."

"When's the time?" Uncle Jimmy wondered out loud. "All those people was there watching us. If that's not the place to say what she said, then when should she say it?"

Aunt Cheryl was undeterred. "Zahra, you asked me what you were supposed to say at a eulogy. I told you what I thought, and then we looked it up together. Remember?"

Zahra did remember. Her speech was supposed to praise her grandmother. She didn't respond to her aunt.

"We talked about some of the memories you and Mama had," Cheryl recalled. "You said you'd talk about what it was like growing up with your grandmother, some of the life lessons she taught you over the years. What you *told me* you would say sounded perfect. What happened to all of that?"

Zahra shrugged. She couldn't meet her eyes – any of them. "When I got up there," she replied, speaking softly, "I forgot what I wanted to say. I was just thinking about how Granny didn't deserve to be there, to get killed like that."

"No one wants to hear about how somebody got killed at their funeral," Cheryl stated. "And talking about that *white man* – that was not the time. We're supposed to be honoring *Mama*, not thinking about some crazy man."

"Cheryl," Sandra said to her sister, "if you think that wasn't the time to do what Zahra did, then this ain't the time

22

either. Why don't you let her grieve the way she wants to? We're on our way to put Mama in the ground. This conversation can wait."

Zahra looked up and saw that her mother was crying again. Aunt Cheryl was too.

"Alright, I'ma let it go," Cheryl said. "I'm just saying it now, in case some people want to give their final words at the gravesite…"

"Don't worry, I'm not gon' speak again," Zahra promised.

"It's okay if you talk, I'm just–"

"I'm not," Zahra repeated. "I said what I had to say, and that's it. I feel bad for what I did."

"I ain't trying to make you feel bad."

The family's new matriarch broke her silence. "Leave it be," Aunt Agatha told Cheryl. She sat stoically with both hands in her lap, wearing all black. "Zahra said she was sorry and she know she was wrong. Sandra's right; this ain't the time to come down on this girl."

Although Agatha had come to her defense, her words crushed Zahra. While she was regretful about what she'd done, she never said she was wrong nor did she apologize. Aunt Agatha had condemned her actions in the nicest possible way, but it was still a condemnation. Coming from her grandmother's sister, the mild rebuke hurt more than anything Aunt Cheryl had to say.

∞ ∞ ∞ ∞ ∞ ∞ ∞

Zahra did not speak again at her grandmother's gravesite.

After making it past the initial shock of learning that her grandmother was killed and the subsequent trauma she endured when the police revealed the circumstances surrounding her death, Zahra hoped her emotions had recovered sufficiently enough to allow her to get through the final portion of the funeral without breaking down again. But there's something so *final* and irreversible about watching your loved one being lowered into the ground.

Thankfully there were plenty of strong men there to support her when she could no longer bear the weight of the tragedy. They helped her to a seat, and she watched the remainder of the ceremony in a daze. Her grandmother was one of 18 people murdered in the shooting. Seventeen more families were grappling with the same grief Zahra was experiencing. But still, she felt that her pain was unique. No one had a granny like hers. She wasn't sure how she would navigate the rest of her life or even the rest of the week without her.

After the service, Zahra was approached by three people as she left the gravesite. The first was Reverend Jesse Jackson. He asked if he could pray with her. Zahra nodded, and he took both of her hands in his.

After the prayer, she looked up at him, surprised by how old he was. She knew that was an odd thing to take note of, considering she was holding hands with a legend who knew Dr. Martin Luther King Jr. personally and participated in the Selma to Montgomery civil rights marches, but it was hard not to notice how frail he seemed.

He told her, "Sister, I wanted to talk to you about what you said at the church."

"It's okay," she said, looking into his eyes. "I know I was wrong to do that. I wasn't trying to ruin the service."

"You didn't ruin it," he replied. "I'm sure some folks would rather you didn't speak that way during your grandmother's eulogy, but you didn't ruin it or spoil the service. It was a very beautiful service. From all I've heard, your grandmother was an amazing woman."

Zahra nodded. Her face flushed with heat.

"What I wanted to tell you," the reverend continued, "is we, as a people, have a tendency to allow our hearts to fill with anger when something like this happens to us. I'm sure you've seen the riots that have occurred in recent years. First, we welcome the anger into our hearts, and then we sometimes lash out in anger. The things we do, while they may feel good at the time, are never productive. I understand you want things to change. I believe change is possible. But we must first approach the problem with calm minds and pure hearts. If you allow your grief to manifest as rage, it will eat you up inside. I've seen it happen many times."

Zahra could not dispute his knowledge or his experience. This man had lived through things that were currently in history books.

"Thank you," she told him. "I appreciate that."

"It's okay, sister." He reached into his coat pocket and produced a business card. "If you find yourself struggling with your emotions or you simply want to talk about how to move forward, please give me a call."

Zahra took the card. Even in the midst of one of the darkest moments of her life, she understood that it was an honor to have this man's number. He rubbed and then squeezed her arm before walking away.

The next person to approach her identified himself as a reporter for Channel Six News. A cameraman followed him and positioned himself to catch an impromptu interview.

"Zahra, I heard your passionate remarks at the funeral, and I want you to know that you and your family have our deepest sympathies. Would you like to elaborate on your thoughts about your grandmother's killer?"

Her grandmother's funeral was over. Zahra didn't think she could ruin anything at that point, but she remained cognizant of what her great aunt had said. They were still at the cemetery. He grandmother's casket had not yet been covered with dirt. This was a time to honor Granny's legacy, not air their grievances about the murderer.

Zahra told the man, "I don't have anything to say, other than what I said at the church."

"I understand," the reporter said. "I just wanted to get your take on the racial aspect of these murders. In the past ten years, there have been seven mass shootings with African Americans as the targets and white men as the shooters..."

Zahra almost took the bait then. She had plenty to say on that topic, but she shook her head and began to walk away. "I'm sorry. I don't have anything to add to what I already said."

She had almost made it back to the limousine provided by the funeral home when a third person approached her. This time it was a young black man dressed in a black suit. Zahra had no way of knowing that two months from now she would be seated at a coffee shop with this individual discussing Andrew Johnson's decision to withhold reparations from the freed slaves.

"Hi, Zahra..."

She stopped and faced him, frowning because the stranger knew her name. She didn't reply.

He said, "I'm sorry about what happened to your grandmother. What you said at the church was right. This was a tragedy that should not have happened. White people have been killing us for far too long. You have a right to be upset about it."

He had her full attention now. She blinked away her tears.

"I know it's probably a lot of people who think you shouldn't have spoken that way at the funeral," the stranger continued. "They'll tell you it wasn't the time or the place. But the thing is, they always think it's not the right time or the right place. They say the same thing whenever somebody walks into a school with an assault rifle and shoots up a classroom. *'It's not the right time to talk about gun control.'* *'The democrats are trying to politicize a tragedy.'* Thing about that is, it be the *politicians* saying that. If you can't talk to a *politician* about *politics*, what the hell they there for? It's these same politicians who refused to pass the Emmett Till Anti-Lynching Act until 2022. That was 57 years after the boy was murdered. Waiting on them to do something is one of the worst things we could do."

Zahra nodded. This man was so in tuned to how she was feeling, it gave her goosebumps.

"My name's David," he said. "But my friends call me *Demon*. Can I give you my number? I want you to call me when you feel like you might wanna take action yourself, instead of waiting for someone to solve our problems."

Zahra's eyes widened. She had so many questions – the first being why someone with a biblical name would allow people to call him something that was the antithesis of godly. She didn't ask him that or any of the other questions swirling through her mind. Instead, she reached into her purse and removed her cellphone. She unlocked it before handing it to him. She studied his face while he added his number to her contacts. She sensed there was something dangerous and powerful about this man. By the time he returned her phone, she was sure she would never call him.

She didn't know how to respond to anything he had said, so she simply told him, "Thank you."

He nodded. "I hope to hear from you soon." He then turned and walked away.

∞ ∞ ∞ ∞ ∞ ∞ ∞

Zahra would have to describe the next two months of her life as a series of efforts in futility. Her first failure was an attempt to return to a semblance of the life she had before her grandmother was murdered. After Granny's repast, she was not surprised when a lot of family members returned to her house to console and comfort one another. But Zahra did not understand why some remained there several days later. The only one who spent the night *every night* was her mother.

On day four, Zahra asked her directly, "Mama, why are you still here?"

Sandra appeared confused and hurt by the question. "I'm here for you, Zahra. I didn't want you to be in this house all by yourself. I can see you slipping into depression. This isn't something you should try to handle by yourself."

Zahra would've preferred if she'd asked rather than assumed, but it may not have mattered either way. Sandra believed she was being helpful, and she would not be deterred.

At least that's what Zahra thought at first.

She later came to believe that her mother was setting herself up to stake claim to her mother's property. Her brothers and sisters quickly followed suit. At first Zahra's aunts and uncles came and took small things. They were always respectful. Zahra had lived there for the past seventeen years, so they would ask her, "Do you mind if I take this with me?" or "You know Mama would want me to have this. You don't mind if I take it, do you?"

Zahra felt it was immature of her to see her relatives as vultures. Their mother was dead, and they had a right to certain keepsakes. When the conversation moved to what they should do with the house, Zahra told them it was too soon to be discussing such things. Her grandmother had only been gone for a month.

"I know you feel like this is your home," Uncle Jimmy told her, "and nobody's saying you have to leave. But eventually, I think we should sell this house. It won't happen right away – not until you decide you want to leave. You can take as long as you want."

In lieu of a will, Zahra knew the beneficiaries of her grandmother's estate were her three children. Zahra looked up the property on Zillow and saw that it was worth $150,000. The only thing standing between her mother, uncle and aunt splitting that pot was Zahra. She considered staying there out of spite, maybe getting married and raising her children there. She might have carried out that plan if not for her mother, who still had not returned to her apartment.

Thirty-two days after her grandmother's death, Zahra began to pack her belongings.

Her mother walked into her bedroom one afternoon and asked, "What are you doing?"

Zahra barely looked at her. "What does it look like? I'm leaving."

After a pause, Sandra asked, "Why? Where are you going?"

"Why does it matter where I go?"

"Why are you getting an attitude with me?"

Zahra almost told her exactly how she felt about her, but she still had a little respect for the woman who birthed her. "I'm moving into an extended stay, until I can get an apartment."

"Why don't you stay here until you get an apartment?"

"Because I don't like what's going on here since Granny died." She looked up at her with tears and malice in her eyes. "I don't like all these people here every day, taking Granny's stuff."

"These people are your relatives."

"And I don't like living with you," Zahra continued.

Sandra opened her mouth and then closed it, holding back her initial response. "You know what, I'ma walk out of here. I know you're upset, and you're saying things you don't mean."

Zahra returned to her packing. She thought that was the end of it, but her uncle walked into the room an hour later.

"What's this I hear about you leaving?"

Zahra didn't have any animosity towards this man, but he wasn't one of her favorite people at the moment. "I am," she told him.

He leaned against the doorframe and watched her for a few beats. "Can I ask why?"

"Because it's not the same here without Granny. It's too many bad memories."

That wasn't the whole truth, but her response had enough truth to make her sound convincing.

"I understand that," Uncle Jimmy said. "Your mama said you're going to an extended stay. Do you wanna come live with me and Deborah, until you get everything straightened out? If you wanna get an apartment, you can live with us until you find one."

She shook her head. "No. I wanna be by myself."

"I don't think that's a good idea. Look, Zahra, I know how much pain you feeling. You probably feel like you're hurting the most, but all of us loved Mama. This a time when family needs to stick together. You shouldn't be over here bickering with yo mama. You shouldn't be going off to live by yourself either. An extended stay ain't no good place for a single woman. All the ones I know about are filled with homeless people and crackheads."

"I found a nice one in Crowley. I didn't see any homeless people when I went to check it out yesterday."

He sighed. "Are you gonna keep in touch?"

"Yeah. You got my number. You can call whenever you want."

"Well, is there anything I can do to help?"

"Sure. I'm almost done packing the things I need for now. You can help me take this stuff to my car in a few minutes."

∞ ∞ ∞ ∞ ∞ ∞ ∞

Zahra had $1,500 to her name. The extended stay charged $450 a week. She could easily pay that amount with the paychecks she received from her job at CVS *if* she managed to keep the job. They waited three weeks after her grandmother's death before they called and inquired about when she might be returning. Zahra told them she wasn't sure. They called again two weeks later, and she gave the same response. She returned to work a week after that, simply to break the monotony of doing nothing all day, but her energy level and zest for the job no longer existed. She wasn't sure if she'd ever liked the job or if she pursued the career at her grandmother's urging.

In the meantime, she'd been trying to start a grassroots organization of some sort that would change the world. Her goal was to stop racist white people from killing black people. Aside from the goal, she had no idea where to start. She had generated a little buzz when the news channels ran footage of her eulogy, but that was several news cycles ago. Since then, the country had experienced two more mass shootings, and a conflict in Europe threatened to pull America into another world war. At the very least, Zahra wanted to gather enough people to protest white supremacists, but she had no idea how to do that either. Everyone she spoke to half-heartedly said they'd be willing to join a protest if she got enough people involved, but she never did.

Sixty-two days after her grandmother's death, Zahra left work at 8pm and stopped at the liquor store on the way home. Knowing she'd regret her plans for the night if she proceeded on an empty stomach, she also stopped at Burger King and got a Whopper combo. An hour later, she had insulated her belly with a full meal. An hour after that, her pint of Patrón was half empty.

She knew it was foolish to drink alone in a hotel room far away from friends and family. It was even more foolish to look up media coverage about the Walmart shooting while drinking alone in a hotel room, but she couldn't stop herself from doing either. Thanks to her iPhone, the internet and YouTube, she found everything she was looking for that night. She even found a clip of her stupid eulogy.

Somebody needs to do something about this. If y'all care about us, like y'all keep saying y'all do, then y'all need to do something to make them stop killing us! I'm sick of it!

Zahra laughed at herself. And talked to herself.

"Bitch, don't nobody give a fuuuuuck," she said to the emotional idiot on her phone. Michael Jackson had been right in 1996. "They don't care about us. You stupid for thinking they do."

By midnight, she had completely drained her bottle of liquor. She felt like complete shit. She understood that she was following in the footsteps of her mother – seeking to relieve emotional trauma with substances. It took her mother fifteen years to realize this was a horrible idea. It only took Zahra one night. It was foolish to leave her grandmother's house. She needed people. She needed someone to care about her. She needed someone to not only tell that her it would be okay but to do something to make things okay.

She stumbled to her suitcase and rummaged through it, looking for the card she'd received from Reverend Jesse Jackson. Halfway through the search, she caught herself. She was drunk, but not drunk enough to call an important man like that while drunk. She sat on her bed and found a different number in her phone. She probably shouldn't call this man either, but she didn't know anything about him. All she knew was that he was the most understanding person she talked to on a horrible day.

He answered after a couple of rings. "Hello?"

"Hey," she said, sitting up straight. "I, um... Is this *David*?"

"Who is this?"

"Zahra."

"Oh. I met you at your grandmother's funeral."

"Yeah, um, can I ask you something?"

"Sure..."

"Why, why you want people to call you *Demon*? Yo mama gave you a Christian name. Are you the devil?"

After a pause, he said, "How much have you had to drink?"

Zahra suddenly felt self-conscious, completely naked. "Why you ask me that?"

"Listen," he said. "It sounds like you not doing too good. I want to help you, but you need to get some sleep and call me in the morning when you're sober."

"You said I could call you if I wanted to talk."

"Yes, I know what I said. What I said is true. But I'm not going to have this conversation until you're sober. If you wanna talk to me, sleep that shit off and call me in the morning."

He disconnected.

Zahra felt like a complete failure.

She cried herself to sleep that night.

In the morning, she took a shower, brushed her teeth, and then she called the man back.

CHAPTER THREE
KING DAVID

"Hello. Zahra?"

"Yes," she said. "It's me."

"How you feeling?" he asked. "Last night you didn't sound so good."

"I'd been drinking. Sorry I called you like that."

"It's okay. Everyone has their good days and bad." He then asked, "Do you drink a lot?"

"No." She shook her head, which made her feel like her brain was bouncing around her skull. The pain made her grit her teeth. "I probably drink once or twice a year. Wish I hadn't done it last night."

"I know you're going through some things," he said. "What's been going on with you, since I saw you at the funeral?"

"A bunch of nothing," she said. "To be honest, I don't know where my life is headed right now..."

She told him about her mother, what had been happening at her grandmother's house and her subsequent decision to move out. She told him how hard it was to return to work and how the job no longer interested her. She told him about her half-assed attempt at activism that never gained any traction. When she was done speaking, she was surprised by the thing Demon chose to comment on.

"I think you need to allow your mother to make amends."

Startled, she asked him, "Why do you feel that way?"

"I know from experience that parents don't always make the right decisions when it comes to their children. My father wasn't in my life when I was coming up. He showed up in the ninth hour and tried to establish a relationship with me. I was bitter. I was resentful. I considered what he'd done and why he did it. I didn't need him anymore, but he needed me. I think my decision was harder than yours. My pops left us to be with another woman and start another family. You said your mother was strung out."

"That was her decision. She chose to do drugs."

"I know it seems like an easy choice, but anyone who's ever been addicted will tell you it's not that simple."

"You did drugs before?"

"No."

She didn't question where his insight came from or say whether she would forgive her mother. Instead she asked, "Why do you want people to call you *Demon. David* was a king in the bible."

"I can see that's something you're really curious about."

"That would be like if my mama named me *Jesus*, but I went by *Satan*. You wouldn't be curious?"

"In the Bible, David was anointed," Demon said. "He was the king of Israel. But he wasn't without his faults. You know he fell in love with Bathsheba, knew she was married, slept with her anyway, got her pregnant, and then tried to trick her husband into sleeping with her, so they could say the baby was his. When that didn't work, David had her husband killed and then married Bathsheba. As a punishment for their sin, they lost their first child."

Zahra knew a little about that story, but she'd never heard it summed up so concisely. "So you don't like to go by David because he was a sinner?"

"No, that's not it. David repented and God forgave him and continued to bless him for the rest of his life. My point is just because you have a biblical name doesn't mean you're anointed. Everyone in the bible, aside from Jesus, was a sinner."

"You still haven't said why you would rather be called *Demon*."

"Everyone in my group has a nickname," Demon explained. "In most cases, we chose something that fits our personality."

Zahra felt goosebumps rise on her arms. She wanted to know what type of group he was involved in and what aspect of his personality he considered demonic. She was afraid to ask about either.

"I'm traveling to Texas in a couple of days," he told her. "Do you want to meet me somewhere?"

Zahra wasn't sure why he wanted to meet with her or if, after what he'd just told her, doing so was in her best interest. But she didn't hesitate. "Yeah, I wanna see you again."

"Okay. I'll give you a call when I'm in town."

∞ ∞ ∞ ∞ ∞ ∞ ∞

37

For the next couple of days, Zahra felt more energized than she had in the past two months, since her grandmother was killed. She wasn't sure why she was so excited about meeting Demon again. Even after speaking to him on the phone, he remained as mysterious as he was when he approached her at her grandmother's gravesite. She was more productive at work. She even took his words into consideration when she stopped by her grandmother's house one evening to pick up more of her things.

Her mother was still there, along with her aunt Cheryl. Zahra saw that more things had been removed from the home – larger items now. Zahra didn't fool herself into believing a relative wanted her grandmother's living room suite for sentimental reasons. She knew they were clearing out the house in preparation for selling it. She was not bothered that they had begun this process within days of her moving out.

"Hey, Zahra," her mother called from the kitchen. "You come to say hi, or you left something behind."

"Getting more of my stuff," Zahra said as she entered the kitchen. "But I can do both."

"I'm making dinner," her mother said, "fried chicken. You got time to eat?"

Zahra didn't have to do anything that night but return to her lonely hotel room. She told her, "Sure."

"I'll be done in about twenty minutes."

"Okay. I'll go pack another bag while you're cooking."

An hour later they were mostly done with the meal, which was actually pretty good. Zahra's mom was not as good a cook as Granny, but Zahra realized she'd missed out on a lot of good cooking, having grown up without her mother in her life. They didn't talk much during the meal.

Aunt Cheryl left shortly afterwards, and Zahra remained at the table.

When they were alone, her mother asked her, "How's things going at your new place? You like living alone?"

Zahra shrugged. "No. Not really."

"But you like it better than living with me..."

Zahra watched her eyes. Her mother was a strong woman. That was shown by her ability to get clean and turn her life around. Despite her strength, she was filled with insecurities, especially when it came to her daughter.

"I'm sorry I told you that," Zahra said. "I was mad 'cause Granny's gone, and everything started changing so fast. I shouldn't have took it out on you."

Sandra was taken aback. That may have been the first time Zahra ever apologized to her. She said, "It's alright. We all handle our emotions differently."

"I wanted to ask you something," Zahra said.

Her mother was all ears.

"What was it like being on drugs," Zahra asked, "and how did you get clean?"

Sandra frowned. "Why you wanna talk about that?"

"I don't know. I was talking to somebody, and they said I don't know what it was like for you, so I shouldn't be mad about what you did."

Sandra continued to knit her eyebrows. "Somebody like who? A counselor?"

Zahra shook her head. "No. Just a friend."

"It..." Sandra sighed. "It's not something that's easy to explain. At first, it starts out kinda fun, like when you first start smoking weed. It feels good to be high. You think everything is better. I know you smoked weed before. Granny told me she caught you getting high a few times."

39

That was true. Zahra hung out with a few smokers during her senior year of high school.

"Once I started getting into *hard* drugs," her mother continued, "it stopped being fun. The high was way more intense, way more addictive. By the time I realized how messed up I was, I was leaving you at home at night, coming back at five or six in the morning. You wasn't nothing but five years old. Anything could've happened to you. But that high I was looking for was more important than caring for you. That's how powerful it is."

Zahra nodded. She wasn't hurt by what she was hearing. She'd heard the story in various forms from other relatives.

"After I gave you to your grandmother," Sandra said, "it was downhill from there. I didn't have no responsibilities. I mean, you was always my responsibility," she backtracked. "But I knew you was somewhere safe, getting fed and clothed and going to school every day. What I did was selfish, but I wasn't thinking straight. I wasn't thinking straight for the next thirteen years." She shook her head.

"That last time I went to rehab, I knew that if I left before I was done with drugs, I might as well kill myself, because I was gon' end up dying anyway. So, I stayed there a whole year. I ain't touched no drugs since the day I walked in that place. I don't drink no alcohol, either."

Zahra continued to nod. She had hoped her mother would've said she decided to get clean for her children, but she didn't fault her for being honest.

"So, this friend of yours," Sandra said, "did they say what hearing this story was supposed to do for you?"

"Just help me understand," Zahra said. "And find some way to forgive you."

Sandra's eyes filled with tears. She swallowed. "Well, do you forgive me?..."

Zahra reached across the table and held her hand. "I know the Christian thing to do is for me to say yes, but I'm not gon' lie to you. Losing Granny made me think about what you did to me even more. I think I can forgive you, one day. Until then, I want you to know that I don't hate you. You gon' always be my mama. I love you."

The tears rolled down Sandra's cheeks. "I love you too, baby. I understand what you saying, and I know it's gon' take some time to fix what I did. I'm just asking that you give me a chance."

Zahra nodded and then rose to her feet, eager to end this conversation. "Do you have any chicken left?" she asked, looking towards the oven. "I wanna take some back to my hotel with me."

"Yeah," Sandra said nodding. She stood and wiped her eyes with the back of her hands. "I'll, uh, I'll make you a plate."

∞ ∞ ∞ ∞ ∞ ∞ ∞

Two days after she last spoke to Demon, Zahra became anxious, wondering if this was the day he would call, and if she should call him if he didn't. When he didn't call by ten p.m. that night, she fought the urge to check on him. She hadn't felt this way since she first started talking to her last boyfriend.

On day three he called while she was getting ready for work. Zahra felt like her heart shot up her throat and began to rattle there.

She had to ask herself, *What the hell is going on?*

She took the phone to the front room and sat on the couch before she answered it.

"Hello."

"Hey, Zahra."

"Hi. You back in Texas?"

"Yeah. I'm in Dallas right now. What you got going on today?"

"I was getting ready to go to work."

"What time you get off?"

"Not till late. The pharmacy closes at eight. I usually have to stay about thirty minutes after that."

"Alright. You working tomorrow?"

"Yeah. I go in at three."

"Wanna meet around ten tomorrow morning?"

"Okay. Where?"

"You drink coffee? We can find a Starbucks or something close to you."

Zahra did drink coffee with her grandmother from time to time, but it had never been a beverage she needed to have. In all twenty-two years of her life, she had never stepped foot in a Starbucks.

"Okay," she told him. "That's cool."

The next morning, Demon called and asked where her hotel was located. She gave him the address. He told her to hold on. Twenty seconds later, he gave her the address of a Starbucks that was less than ten minutes away.

An hour later, she had barely sipped her caramel macchiato as she and Demon sat across from each other and discussed the reasons white supremacists hated blacks and sometimes decided to murder them. Just when Zahra began to feel dejected by the conversation – Demon had all the answers but had provided no solution to the problem – he surprised her by saying, "I didn't say there was nothing we could do about it, Zahra. I never said that..."

This was what Zahra had been waiting months to hear from him, since the day she laid her grandmother to rest. But Demon didn't elaborate on that statement while they were at Starbucks. Instead, he switched gears.

He told her, "There's someone I want you to meet. He's a prisoner. Would you mind traveling to Huntsville with me? I can get you on his visitor's list."

Confused, Zahra asked, "Who? Why do you want me to meet a prisoner?"

"He's a white supremacist," Demon said without batting an eye. "He murdered three black men at a bar, about ten years ago. You might have heard about it..."

Zahra frowned. "I don't want to meet anyone like that. Why do you want me to?"

"If you want me to help you," he said, "if you want to do something to help our people, it's important for you to know what type of people we're up against. I understand it will be uncomfortable for you to meet this man, but I don't think we can move forward unless you do."

Zahra didn't think it was possible to be more perplexed about the man she was speaking to. With each encounter, she was able to peel back another layer of his personality, but she didn't think she would ever understand his thought process.

"Alright, I'll do it," she breathed.

He nodded. "Good. I'll reach out to him. It usually takes a couple of weeks to get someone new on his visitor's list. I'll reach out to you when it's done." He stood and looked down at their table. "You gonna finish that coffee?"

She shook her head and stood as well. "No. I don't like it. It's too sweet."

They left the coffee shop and headed to two different vehicles. Zahra didn't like the idea of waiting two weeks before she'd hear from him again, but this was Demon's show, and he alone was setting the rules of engagement.

CHAPTER FOUR
GERALD LEE HENRY

The following Friday, Zahra received a call from a good friend from high school. Stacy came to her grandmother's funeral, but the two hadn't spoken much in the months prior to that. Stacy wanted to know if Zahra wanted to hit the clubs that night.

"I'm not really feeling the clubs right now," Zahra told her. "But we can go to the mall tomorrow. I didn't realize how old my clothes were until I started packing so I could move."

The next day, they met at Hulen Mall. For Zahra, it felt good to be out, doing something *normal* for a change. Between visiting stores and taking outfits to the dressing rooms, Zahra told her friend about how much her life had changed since her grandmother was murdered. Stacy was a good listener. She offered her condolences, promising things would get better. But it was Zahra's new acquaintance that Stacy was most curious about.

"You told him you would go?" she asked, regarding Demon's invitation to visit a killer in prison.

"Yeah. I don't want to, but he made it sound like he can't help me unless I do it."

"Girl, let's go over here. Sit down." Stacy led her to a lounge area near the food court. Once seated, she watched her friend with concern and compassion battling for dominance in her features. "Help you *how*, Zahra? What do you think he can do for you?"

She shook her head. "I don't know. When I met him at the funeral, he said I could call him when I was ready to do something – *take action*, was the way he put it. He said he could help if I was sick of waiting around for someone to solve this problem."

"The problem of white people killing blacks?"

Zahra nodded. "Yeah."

"Did he say what he could do to help solve that problem?"

Zahra shook her head.

"But he thinks you need to meet some killer in prison before he can help you..."

She nodded.

"And his name is *Demon* – or at least that's what he wants to be called?"

Still nodding, Zahra said, "Yeah."

"Did he say why he wants to be called that?"

"He said everyone in his group uses a name that matches their personality."

"Did he tell you anything about his group?"

"No."

Exasperated, Stacy said, "Zahra, I shouldn't have to be the one to tell you none of this makes sense. I guess I can understand him not volunteering any of this information, but I don't understand why you ain't asking him these

46

questions. You're willing to get in the car with this person –
this *stranger* – and drive all the way to Huntsville. This man
could be dangerous, for all you know."

Actually, Zahra already felt Demon was a dangerous
individual. This was one of the reasons she hadn't told
anyone in her family about him. Stacy's opinion didn't hold
as much weight as someone like Uncle Jimmy.

"I'm willing to take my chances," she told her friend.
"Demon is smart. I feel like he knows what he's doing.
Whenever I'm around him, I'm not getting any vibes like he
wants to hurt me."

"Maybe not," Stacy said. "But you gotta admit this
whole thing is bizarre."

"Is it? I think it's bizarre for some random white dude
to drive from his *white* neighborhood to my *black*
neighborhood and walk in a store and start killing folks. I
think it's bizarre for someone to see my Granny, as old as she
was and as sweet as she was, and stick a rifle in her face and
pull the trigger – for no fucking reason at all. And kill
seventeen more black people, while he's at it. For something
like that to happen out of the blue, for it to *keep* happening,
even at a church – I think that's way more bizarre than a
man named Demon asking me to go to prison to meet a
white supremacist."

At some point during her spiel, Zahra's demeanor had
shifted, as quickly and drastically as someone pulling the
shades down. Stacy saw that her friend's eyes were glossy,
but they were also resilient. She'd never seen Zahra so fierce
and determined.

"I'm sorry for what happened to your grandmother,"
she said. "She didn't deserve that. None of them did. I just

want you to be careful. I don't know what this man has in store for you. I don't want you to get hurt."

"If I get hurt, but I also prevent another tragedy from happening, I'ma take that as a win."

Stacy didn't agree with that proposition, but she sensed she'd only drive a wedge between them if she continued arguing, so she let it go for now.

∞ ∞ ∞ ∞ ∞ ∞ ∞

Sixteen days after Zahra met Demon at Starbucks, he called again.

"Hey, what's up, you busy?"

"No," she said. "I'm off today, just running some errands."

"I got approval for you to go to the prison with me. You busy tomorrow?"

Tomorrow was Saturday. Zahra knew her boss would not approve a call-out for a weekend shift, but she told him, "No. I'm supposed to work, but I can take off."

"You sure?"

"Yeah. We're going to Huntsville?"

"If you didn't change your mind..."

"No, I didn't."

"Okay. I usually like to leave early when I head out there, so I won't feel like it took the whole day. It's about a three-hour drive."

"You go there a lot?"

"More than I'd like to. Is it cool if I pick you up at seven?"

Zahra couldn't remember the last time she'd been up and ready to go at that hour. Since graduating high school, she purposefully took second shift jobs to avoid the morning bustle. But she told him, "Yeah, that's cool. I'll be ready."

∞ ∞ ∞ ∞ ∞ ∞ ∞

The next morning, he called at 7am sharp. "I'm downstairs, parked outside the office."

"Alright. I'm on my way."

Due to daylight savings time, the sun was already rising in the eastern skies at that hour. For now, the mid-June temperature was pleasant. The high was expected to reach 92 degrees. When she exited the hotel, Zahra spotted the black Charger she'd seen Demon driving when he met her at Starbucks. She approached the vehicle and got in on the passenger side.

He gave her a once-over as she sat down and fastened her seatbelt. Demon wore jeans and a tee-shirt. Zahra was similarly dressed.

He asked her, "How you been?" as he backed out of his parking space.

"I been okay."

"Thanks for agreeing to meet this guy. I know you're probably looking for a method to my madness. Things will start making sense after today. I promise."

She nodded. "I'm sure it will. I trust you."

He looked over at her. "Really?"

"Yeah. I mean, I'm allowing you to drive me three hours away from home, and none of my family members know where I'm going or who I'm going with. That's trust, right?"

"You haven't told anyone about me?"

"Only one of my friends."

49

"Why not your family?"

"What am I supposed to tell them, some *Demon* wants to take me to meet a man who killed some black people. How's that conversation supposed to go?" she asked with a smirk.

He chuckled. "I see your dilemma. In my defense, you haven't asked a lot of questions."

"I figured you'd tell me what I needed to know when you decided it was time to tell me."

He nodded. "What about the guy we're going to see? You got any questions about him?"

"I guess you could start with his name."

"Gerald Henry. Look him up. We're gonna be on the road for a while. You should do some research."

Zahra did. She learned that Gerald Lee Henry was a Dallas native. On the evening of October 8th, 2011, Gerald visited a bar called Fire Lounge with two cousins. At approximately one a.m. the trio got into a physical altercation with another group of men, all of whom were black. Witnesses and surveillance footage indicated the second trio got the better of Gerald's group, but no one was seriously injured. All six men were asked to leave the establishment. The bar's manager did not call police at that time.

Less than five minutes after the men left the bar, patrons heard a volley of gunfire in the parking lot. A witness reported, "It sounded like a machine gun." The police were called this time. When they arrived, they found all three black men suffering from gunshot wounds. One was pronounced deceased at the scene. The other two died shortly after arriving at the hospital. Gerald's group had fled the scene, but based on a witness' description of their vehicle, they were found later that night. All three men were arrested and charged with murder.

During the trial, both of Gerald's cousins testified that he had fired all of the fatal shots with an assault rifle he retrieved from the trunk of his car. The prosecutors also uncovered evidence that painted Gerald out to be a racist, which they used as a possible motive for the murders. Zahra read about a slew of racial incidents Gerald had been involved in, including harassing a black family that moved in across the street from his mother's home. In that incident, Gerald hung a black-faced effigy from a noose on a tree in his mother's front yard. Gerald also taped a confederate flag to his mother's front window (facing the neighbor's home) and wrote the word NIGGER under the flag.

Gerald never admitted to firing his weapon that night, but ballistic evidence proved his rifle was the murder weapon. Forensic evidence revealed his DNA was the only one on the weapon. A gunshot residue test proved he had fired a gun on the night of the murders. Gerald was convicted of the triple murder and was sentenced to serve three life sentences that would run consecutively. He would never be released from prison. In return for their cooperation and the district attorney's belief that they did not participate in the murders, Gerald's cousins were convicted of manslaughter. These charges were sought because they did not call the police to report a crime they had witnessed. They both received ten-year sentences.

After her research, Zahra was curious about Demon's connection with the case.

"How do you know this man, and why is he okay with you visiting him in prison? I know he doesn't like black people."

"Gerald and I have a hate/hate relationship," Demon revealed. "I know he doesn't like me, and he knows I don't like him. When I first contacted him, I was *mostly* honest. I told him I wanted to know why someone like him did what they did. I wanted to know where his hate originated. I told him I was a psychology student, doing a paper on race relations."

"He believed you?"

"I don't know if he did or not. He refused to see me at first. He wrote me some pretty nasty letters. Called me all kinds of niggers. But I was persistent. Plus I started putting money on his books. Finally, he agreed to see me."

"*You pay him?*" Zahra was shocked.

Demon nodded. "Yup. Fifty bucks a month every month. He may not be able to trust anything or anyone right now, but he knows my money is coming every month on the exact same day."

"I can't believe you would do that, after what he did."

"I told you, I needed to understand who I was up against. Plus, every now and then I meet someone like you, and I need to let you know who you're up against. I can tell you how bad these people are, but there are some things you need to see for yourself. I tried to bring a few people in without requiring that they meet Gerald first. Shit didn't go well."

"Bring me into what, Demon?" For the first time since she'd met him, Zahra was worried about what she was getting herself into.

"Let's get through this meeting first," he replied. "Everything will be easier to swallow after you meet Gerald. You said you trust me, right?"

She was frowning, but she nodded. "Yeah."

He nodded. "Okay then. Let that be the reason..."

∞ ∞ ∞ ∞ ∞ ∞ ∞

After stopping for breakfast to go, they arrived at the prison at 10:30. Zahra hated the place the moment she laid eyes on it. Barbed wire, concrete, thousands of men suffering inside. After receiving a life sentence for murder, her father had been doing time in a unit like this for the past twenty years. Zahra didn't visit him often. She barely knew the man. Each time she did visit, the experience left her with a bad taste in her mouth. She hated the waiting once she got inside. She hated having her person and her belongings searched by individuals who chose to house human beings for a living. She hated the opposite emotions on display when she talked to her father through a thick glass: He was always ecstatic that she had come to see him, while she immediately began to count down the hour until their visit would end.

The visitation process at Huntsville was the same as Ferguson Unit, where her father was caged. By the time she and Demon made it to a large room with a large glass cubicle in the center, Zahra was on edge. Inside the cubicle were ten inmates dressed in prison garb. They all sat facing the glass. On the opposite side, the visitors sat around the cubicle, with about six feet between them. A guard stood in each corner of the room. These visits did not allow for much privacy, but that was just as well. Zahra didn't expect to have an intimate moment with the white man Demon led her to and took a seat across from. Zahra sat next to him.

Gerald folded his massive arms over his chest and grinned at Demon. He looked over at Zahra and continued

53

to smile. She did not smile back. She studied him, took in his muscular physique, bald head and the tattoos on his arms, neck and head. She didn't know a lot about white supremacist tats, but she didn't have to. It was easy to follow a roadmap of his beliefs written on his leathery skin. His forearms proudly proclaimed he was a RED NECK, with one word on each arm. A double lightning bolt on his neck was reminiscent of Hitler's paramilitary SS troops. If anyone was still unsure of his affiliation, the numbers 14 and 88 on his forehead provided the last piece of the puzzle. Eighty-eight referenced the eighth letter of the alphabet twice. In this case *Heil Hitler*. Fourteen referred to fourteen words that were fundamental to most white supremacist groups: *We must secure the existence of our people and a future for white children.*

Gerald had a large handlebar moustache and was missing one of his front teeth. Zahra hoped a black inmate had knocked it out. She despised this man before he opened his mouth to greet them.

"David," Gerald said, using his government name. "I see you brought another one..."

"Yeah. How you been?" Demon asked.

"Can't complain," Gerald said. He turned his attention to Zahra. "She's pretty. I can already tell she don't like me."

"Nobody likes you," Demon said.

Gerald laughed at that.

"Do you mind telling my friend what you're locked up for?" Demon prompted.

Gerald shook his head, still grinning. "You know I don't mind reliving the best night of my life. Did you bring some quarters?"

"Of course I did," Demon said, showing him a cup he received during the visitor intake. It was full of shiny coins.

"Why don't you go get me some snacks?" Gerald asked. "Make me feel like I'm watching a good movie, if I have something to snack on while we talk."

"I'll be back in a second," Demon said.

Zahra watched him walk to a vending machine. She wanted to throw up.

Demon purchased three bags of chips and two Snickers bars. He gave the treats to a guard who entered the area where the prisoners sat and delivered the gift to Gerald. With his snacks secured, Gerald tore into the wrappings one by one and proceeded to tell the whole story while he chomped down. He was polite enough to avoid using the N-word, but he couldn't hide his disdain for blacks while he spoke. It was clear he relished the memory of October 8th. He seemed to particularly enjoy Zahra's discomfort.

Towards the end, he told her, "Now I know you're probably thinking I went too far. But here's the deal: This is a white man's world. The day a black man thinks he can rise up and raise his hand to a white man is the day that black man has to be put down, like any dog that would bite its master. I shot 'em, all three of 'em, all by myself. The only regret I have about that night is I should've killed more blacks. If I knew I was gonna get caught so quickly, I would've drove to one of those black clubs and laid 'em all down. Anyway, that's why I'm here."

Zahra looked around at the other prisoners in the tank with him. None of them were paying attention to the filth he was spewing.

Demon let everything Gerald had said sink in before asking, "What do you think about Patrick Wood Crusius?"

Zahra didn't know the name, but Gerald smiled.

"Good man," he said. "A true soldier. That's how you get something done. What was his body count?" he asked Demon. "Twenty-two, twenty-three?"

"Twenty-three Latinos," Demon said.

"Yeah," Gerald said. "That's how you get it done."

"What about Dylann Roof?" Demon asked.

Gerald rolled his eyes slightly, still smiling. "Come on, David. These are easy questions. You already know how I feel about him."

"I'm not asking for me. I want you to tell my friend."

Zahra didn't want that at all. She was sick of the deranged man looking and speaking directly to her.

"Dylann Roof is a soldier," Gerald told her. "See, the thing about him is he knew it's not just how many you kill but *who* you kill. He took out the senior pastor, who just happened to be a *state senator*. That's how you do it. That's how you make a statement."

"What do you think about the white people out there who haven't killed any black people yet, but they're making plans to. If someone like me or maybe the police could reach them and try to talk them out of it *before* it happens, what could we say to make them change their minds about the way they feel about black people?"

Gerald shook his head. "You got a better chance teaching a horse to use a litter box. People like that, people like me, we ain't gon' change our mind until *you people* get the hell out of our country – and take the Mexicans with you. I know you're not gonna do that, though. You're gonna sit around and keep taking from us until the race war pops off. Once you see we mean business, you'll rethink your position on how bad you wanna stay in this country."

Demon nodded. If he was bothered by any of this, it didn't show.

"One last question," he said. "What do you think about Brandon Guillory?" He didn't have to look over at Zahra to feel her stiffen next to him.

Gerald's eyes lit up. "Oh, that's the new one. Another true soldier. If something like that happened every week, I don't think it would take long for one of two things to happen."

"What are those two things?"

"Either y'all decide it ain't worth trying to stay in America, or y'all decide to fight back. That's really what we're hoping will happen. When you fight back, we'll wipe y'all out of every hood and ghetto."

Demon checked on Zahra. Her breath had become a little labored. Her eyes were glossy. She continued to stare at the inmate, unblinking. Gerald noticed it too.

"Seems like I hit a soft spot."

"Her grandmother was in that Walmart," Demon informed him. "The one Guillory attacked."

"Aww hell," Gerald said. "You set me up."

"Does knowing that her grandmother was one of the victims make you feel any different."

He shook his head. "Not at all."

"She was eighty-two years old," Demon said.

"And that makes a pretty strong statement," Gerald replied. "Don't you think? What that says to me is no matter who you are, no matter how young or how old, if you black, you ain't safe. There's no refuge. There are thousands of people like me in the free world. Tens of thousands. *Hundreds* of thousands."

Zahra spoke for the first time since the visit started. She asked Demon, "Can we leave now?" It took every bit of her resolve to hold it together.

"Yeah," he said. He rose to his feet and helped her to a standing position. Before they walked away, he told Gerald, "I'll see you later."

"Yeah, I'm sure you will. I don't know why," he said to Zahra, "but this guy can't get enough of me."

CHAPTER FIVE
INVASION OF PRIVACY

By the time they got back to Demon's car, Zahra was fuming. She'd told her friend she trusted this man. She didn't think he wanted to do anything to harm her. But that was a lie. What happened during their visitation was extremely hurtful, unnecessarily so.

"Why would you do that?" she breathed. *"Why do you feel like that needed to happen?"* She'd managed to hold her tears in while in the presence of the killer, but they rolled down her cheeks now. Her eyes were wet and red with anger.

Demon remained calm as he exited the prison complex. He effectively shut down her anger with five simple words. "That man killed my uncle."

"Wh, what?" Her eyes remained frantic as she tried to wrap her mind around everything that had transpired.

Demon nodded slowly. "One of the three men Gerald killed on October 8th, 2011 was my uncle. His name is Charles Easton."

The name was familiar. Zahra remembered it from the news stories she read on the way to the prison.

"I know you feel like I just put you through unnecessary trauma," Demon said. "Please understand I would never ask you to do anything I haven't done myself. And, like I told you on the way down here, I believe that was necessary."

Zahra didn't know what to feel at that moment. Her soul was a whirlwind of emotions.

"I – I'm sorry," she said.

He shook his head. "No. I'm sorry he upset you."

But was he really? He had to know how Gerald would respond when he asked about the recent Walmart shooting.

"Does he know that he killed your uncle?" She wiped the tears from her eyes and focused on getting her breathing under control.

"No," Demon said. "When I first reached out to him, it was like I told you. I don't think he would've agreed to it, if he knew I was related to one of his victims. I suppose I could've told you about my uncle before we met Gerald. There's a lot you don't know about me, Zahra. But one thing you need to understand is I didn't get into this fight because I was sick of hearing about all those hashtags. I got into it for the same reason you might decide to get into it – because it affected me personally."

"I think..." She took a deep breath and blew it out slowly. "I think I'm already into this, David."

She did not use his real name on purpose or out of disrespect. He did not ask her not to call him that.

"Since I've come this far," she continued, "are you gonna tell me what it is I'm getting myself into?"

She was disappointed to see him shake his head. "You're not into anything yet. Right now you're at a crossroads. I want you to take some time to decide which way you wanna go. I don't want you to make a decision now, because you're emotional, and your decision will be fueled by your emotions. I can't trust that kind of decision."

She sighed. "How am I supposed to make a decision when I don't know what I'm deciding?"

"I want you to decide what you think should happen to people like Gerald. He's never getting out of prison. Do you think that's a good punishment?"

She shook her head. "No. I think he should be put to death."

"I agree," Demon said. "Tell me why you feel that way."

"I think he doesn't mind being in prison. He still gets to wake up every day, get three free meals. He gets commissary, thanks to you."

Demon rolled his eyes at that. "Is that it?"

"Yeah, I guess. You have more reasons?"

"Yes. I think people like Gerald are *legends* in prison, at least with the Aryan gangs. People who've never killed a black man before live through him. They learn from him. Some of them will be released one day, and when they hit the streets, they'll be worse than Gerald. He should be put to death because he's an influencer, just like those people on TikTok. More black people will probably die because of the influence he has in prison."

Zahra felt like the temperature in the car cooled as she asked her next question. "So, you wanna find some way to kill him in prison?"

Demon surprised her by saying, "No. I don't have enough resources to do something like that. There's no one on the inside I can trust enough to pull that off. I'm more concerned about what we should do with the people like him on the outside. Do you believe what Gerald said, about there being no way to rehabilitate those people?"

Zahra nodded. She sensed they were close to the resolution he promised.

But he switched gears again. He lifted his cellphone and found a page he had bookmarked. "Ever heard of 4chan?" he asked.

Zahra shook her head.

"It's an anonymous internet message board," he explained. "I want you to read something."

He handed her the phone. What Zahra saw was a very long post, written by someone with the screen name "cantreplaceme."

"Do you know what this is?" he asked.

She shook her head.

"It's a manifesto" he informed her. "Recently, a lot of people who commit mass shootings create a manifesto. They usually don't post it until the day they plan to commit their crime. This one was posted thirty minutes before your grandmother's killer walked into the Walmart."

Zahra's body froze.

"If you can't read it, I understand," Demon said. "But it's like I told you, we have to understand why these people do what they do, even if it hurts us to know their justification. Have you ever heard of the book *The Art of War*?"

"I think I heard of it," she said, still not wanting to look at his phone.

"Sun Tzu teaches that if you know your enemy and you know yourself, you will never fear the result of a battle. I told you that you're at a crossroads. You have to decide what you're willing to do, how far you're willing to go. The other half of that is to know your enemy – not just what you've been told about them. That's why I took you to see Gerald, and that's why I read every word of every manifesto one of these white supremacists writes before they attack our people."

Zahra took a deep breath and told him, "Okay."

She read the killer's manifesto. Every word. And she hated it. Every word. She hated how he blamed blacks and other minorities for virtually every problem the country was facing. She hated how he believed murdering people like her grandmother would cause blacks to flee the country in fear. She hated how well he wrote and how coherent he managed to make his inconceivable ramblings sound. Most importantly, she hated how the manifesto could be used as a motivational tool. This was evident by the fact that the killer mentioned another extremist who murdered 51 people in two mosques in New Zealand. The man who killed Zahra's grandmother had read the other killer's manifesto and seemed to be inspired by it.

When she was done reading, she felt as disgusted as she felt while visiting Gerald Lee Henry. "How can this be legal?" she asked Demon. "Why don't they shut this website down?"

"The website exists because of Freedom of Speech," he explained. "There are a lot of racists post, but until they rise to the level of threatening violence, it's protected speech. It's not illegal for someone to go online and say *I hate niggers*. As far as the manifesto, that's not protected speech, because he said he wanted to do something violent. But, like I said, these killers don't post their manifesto until it's too late to stop them."

"So, what are we gonna do about it?" she asked. Her nostrils flared. "I'm ready."

Demon gave her a long look before his eyes returned to the road. "Zahra, this is as far as I can go with you, until you go home and take some time to think about everything I've said and everything that's happened. If you want to be a part of what my group is doing, you need to understand that your life will never be the same afterwards. I'll be in the Dallas area for a few days. After that, I'm catching a flight. I want you to come with me. If you decide to do so, I can't say when or if you'll ever return home. I can't promise that you'll always be safe. Don't make a decision now. If you decide you want to come with me, get your affairs in order and be ready to leave when I call you. Do you understand?"

She did. And she thought she had a pretty good idea what type of business Demon was into. She was scared, but she was also determined. She knew Demon was cunning and extremely calculating. Despite his warning, she still did not believe he would allow any harm to come to her.

"Okay," she said. "But you better call me in three days."

He gave her another look. "Zahra, I have never told you I was going to do something that I have not done. You never have to worry about me keeping my word."

∞ ∞ ∞ ∞ ∞ ∞ ∞

Demon called exactly three days later. He did not ask if Zahra had made a decision. Instead, he told her, "I know you decided to go with me."

Stunned, she asked, "How do you know that?"

"I'll explain when I get there. I'll pick you up tomorrow at noon. Pack light. We're getting on a plane. You can bring one checked bag and one carry on. You don't need anything other than that."

The hairs stood on her arms. "Oh, okay."

"I'll see you tomorrow," he said and disconnected.

The next day he showed up promptly at twelve p.m. wearing shorts and a tee shirt. He looked like he was on vacation. Zahra knew this trip would be anything but recreation. She invited him inside and stared at him as he crossed the threshold into her hotel room. Demon always had a serious look about him. He never seemed to put too much effort into his appearance, but he was a good-looking man. His face was shaved, other than a thin moustache and a tuft of hair on his chin. He always wore the same three necklaces. They were thin, not gaudy, with a different medallion hanging from each one. He looked around and saw that she had two bags packed, one large, the other small enough to carry onto the plane.

He headed for them, but she stopped him by asking, "How did you know I was going with you? Yesterday you didn't ask me. You said you knew I decided to go."

He turned to face her. He stared into her eyes, which were just as serious as his.

"Zahra, I knew you wanted to go with me just like I knew the personal information needed to get you on Gerald's visitation list. You never asked how I did that, without asking for your date of birth and driver's license number."

Zahra's eyes widened. He was right; she hadn't.

"You also didn't ask how I got you a plane ticket. As far as you know, I don't even know your last name."

She blinked quickly, her mind racing. "So, you do know my last name…"

"Avery," he said. "Date of birth April 14th." He rattled off her driver's license number.

Other than pursing her lips, she didn't respond.

"I know your credit score is 760," he said. "I know you work at CVS – up until yesterday afternoon. You quit, rather than show up for your shift. You have about $1,200 in the bank – Wells Fargo. You don't have an account anywhere else. You only have two bags here, because you took the rest of your belongings to your mother's house yesterday, when you normally would've been at work. Your mother's name is Sandra Pratt. She lives on the east side, on Forbes Street. I know that she dropped you off at this hotel last night, and she's keeping your car indefinitely."

"You followed me?" But Zahra knew it was more than that. Following her wouldn't have revealed her credit score or how much money she had in her account.

"I think by now you know that what I do is serious," he told her. "Everyone in my group is a genius in their own right. The guys we have on the computers can do things I don't even understand. If it bothers you that I did my research on you, and you wanna back out, now is the time to do it. I know I invaded your privacy. I had to do that to protect myself and my people. I'm not apologizing for it."

Zahra's heart began to thud. Her mouth was so dry, she didn't think she could speak. She shook her head and managed to tell him, "No. I don't wanna back out."

His head cocked slightly. "Do you have any idea what you're getting yourself into?"

"I – I think we're gonna kill somebody."

He watched her for what felt like an eternity. Then he said, "Yeah. We are. More specifically, *you* are. Everyone I bring in has to pop their cherry. That's the only way the group will trust you. The man we're killing lives in Georgia. That's where we're headed. You still wanna go?"

Her heart was knocking so hard, she was sure he could hear it or maybe see it through her shirt. She nodded stiffly. "Can, can I ask who we're killing – and why?"

"I think you already know *why*, but I don't have time to get into that right now." He turned and hefted her bags. "Come on. We got a flight to catch."

He exited the hotel. She hesitated, only for a moment, before following him.

CHAPTER SIX
JIM CROW MUST GO

On the way to the airport, Zahra felt like she was all in. Demon must have felt the same way, because she didn't have to inquire again about who they were targeting in Georgia.

"The guy's name is Eric Slater," he told her. "He's twenty-two, lives in John's Creek. We've been tracking him for about six months now. He started out expressing interests in white supremacist groups, like the Proud Boys, Storm Front, American Front. A lot of people express interest in groups like that. Depending on the type of things they post when they visit those websites, they may get put in a database we created. Our computer guys are good enough to get the IP address of their computer. They can also get the IP address of their phone, if that's what they're using most often.

"Eric moved higher up on our list when he started looking into the boogaloo movement. Have you ever heard of that?"

Zahra shook her head, amazed that his *computer guys* had the ability to track someone's IP address.

"The boogaloo movement," Demon explained, "goes by different names, but that's the most common one. Some of the people associated with it call themselves the *boogaloo boys*. Interestingly, they got their name from a black movie, came out in '84. *Breakin' 2: Electric Boogaloo*. But the people in this group, or movement, aren't into dancing. They believe the racial unrest we've been experiencing in this country is gonna lead to a civil war. They already got a name for it – *Civil War 2: Electric Boogaloo*. They wanna use the war to wipe out all the blacks, jews and other minorities. They're training for the war. A lot of them are heavily armed."

Zahra knew she shouldn't be surprised by his intel, but she couldn't help it.

Know your enemy.

"Anyway," he continued, "Eric has been active on a lot of message boards, 4chan being one of them. He hasn't posted anything implicitly saying he was gonna commit an act of violence, but his hate for blacks is off the charts. Plus, he's been doing some things behind the scenes that fall in line with other mass murderers. He's looked up all the manifestos from other white supremacists who carried out their plans. This was enough for us to make the decision to take him out. When we moved to phase 2, physical surveillance, we saw that Eric's been going to the gun range a lot recently. He takes a semi-automatic rifle and a pistol with him. We did more research and learned that he bought the rifle two months ago.

"Eric became priority number one four days ago, when he started writing his own manifesto. He's saving it in

69

Google Drive. If he was saving it in Microsoft Word, we may not have access to it, but with Google Drive it's in the cloud. I've been reading it each day as he adds to it. There's nothing unique about what he's writing. His opinions aren't any different from a thousand other racists. But the more he writes, the more I feel like we're running out of time."

Zahra didn't have a comment when he was done speaking.

He asked her, "Does it make sense to you that we would kill someone who hasn't harmed anyone yet?"

She nodded. It was hard to believe how far removed she was from the values her grandmother had taught her. "Yeah, it does."

"Some would say this man is *innocent*," Demon pressed. "You're okay with taking an innocent man's life?"

"If he's planning to murder some of our people, he's not innocent."

Demon nodded. "I knew you'd feel that way. I knew it from the moment I saw you speak at your grandmother's funeral."

They drove in silence for a while, and then she said, "Can I ask how many times you've done this – you and your group?"

"Not as many times as I would like," he replied. "We've only been active for three years. In that time, we've taken out fifty-two people. Most of them hadn't gone as far as the one we're going after. But I believe we should always err on the side of caution. Even if we were wrong, and some of these guys were all talk – *internet gangstas* – I'm okay with silencing them permanently. These people feed off each other's energy. Constantly talking reckless about what you *wanna* do can inspire someone else to actually do it."

Zahra understood that. "How many people are in your group?" she asked.

"Counting the Mexican, twenty-one."

As serious as this conversation was, she chuckled at that.

"What?" he said.

"*Counting the Mexican.* Are Mexicans not allowed to be in your group?"

"No, it's not that. I just mean he's not fully invested, not like the rest of us. He still has a job and a family he goes home to every day."

"No one in the group has a job?"

Demon shook his head.

"How can you afford to do what you do?"

"You remember I told you that you have about $1,200 in the bank?"

She nodded.

"My computer guys are so good, I could've withdrawn that money and handed it to you when I picked you up today."

Zahra frowned in disbelief.

"But it ain't all about stealing," Demon said. "We got some people who back us, some important people. They down for the cause, but they don't want nobody to know they had anything to do with us, if we ever get caught."

"People like who?"

"I will never tell you that. Let's just say it's some Jews out there who have more money than they know what to do with. They know these white supremacists hate them as much as they hate blacks. And it's some well-off blacks who believe in what we're doing but don't wanna get their hands dirty. I'm talking folks with *Tyler Perry* money."

Zahra mulled that over and was quiet for a while longer. "I was thinking about what you told me."

"What's that?"

"You said there was a lot I don't know about you. I know part of that is because I haven't asked you any personal questions. But you haven't volunteered anything either..."

His eyes narrowed. "What is it you wanna know about me?"

Zahra didn't know where to begin. "You said you're from Dallas. Were you always this smart? What was your life like when you were younger, before you got into this... *movement*?"

He sighed. "There was nothing special about my past. I went to school, had perfect attendance, but I made mostly C's. I played basketball. That was my favorite sport, but I was never too good at it. I made the team each year in high school, but I spent more time on the bench than on the court."

She grinned. "You made mostly C's, as smart as you are?"

"I don't think I'm that smart."

"You said everyone in your group is a genius in their own right."

"Yeah, I did say that. I guess I am smart, when it comes to certain things."

"You know a lot about white supremacists."

"Unfortunately, yeah, I do. Wish I didn't have to study them as much as I do."

"You said you got involved in this because of what happened to your uncle?"

He nodded. "Yeah. That was the tipping point for me, but not till years later. Before that, I guess I was like anybody else. I heard about the murders – not just the mass murders but the way the police are killing us. I cared, but I was never spurred into action until it hit close to home."

Zahra understood that completely.

"I told you my dad wasn't in my life," he said. "My uncle, he was always around. He didn't raise me; I lived with my mother and my brothers and sisters. But my uncle, he came and scooped us kids up, at least once a week. As I grew older, he's the one who taught me how to be a man, what it means to take care of the people in your life. I looked up to him. I loved the shit out of him. When my mama told me he got killed..."

Zahra watched him. He didn't cry, but she was sure his eyes watered.

"I wasn't nothing but thirteen. I knew it was a white man who killed him, and later I found out it was a racial killing. I didn't know how to process all of that. After I graduated high school, I was hearing about more killings, usually the police shooting an unarmed black man. This was before George Floyd, before the Black Lives Matter movement got as big as it did. As an adult, I went back and researched my uncle's murder. I was already pissed, but what I read made me even more mad.

"That's when I decided I wanted to do something. I realized we're at war, and the enemy isn't fighting the same kind of fight as us. We protesting, and them motherfuckers killing us. I studied the Civil Rights Movement. I read a lot. Some of it, I already knew a little about. Some of it was brand new to me. I don't take nothing away from folks like Gandhi, Mandela or Martin Luther King Jr. The way they went about getting change *worked*, so I can't say they was wrong. But for the kind of fight I wanted to fight, I knew

73

their methods wouldn't work for me. Peaceful protests can get a government to change its policies, but no piece of paper a president has ever signed has stopped racist whites from hating us.

"I studied the other black movements that came before us, and that's when I decided that if I was gonna take action, I couldn't do it publicly. What they did to our black leaders in the 50s and 60s was crazy. The more I read, the worse it got. For every martyr you heard of, a hundred more activists got killed. It was Medgar Evers that made me say *Fuck that*. Ain't no way I'm finna take a stand and put a bullseye on my chest."

Zahra had heard that name but knew nothing about him. "What happened to Medgar Evers?"

"He was a standup guy," Demon reflected. "Fought in World War II, was a decorated soldier. Tried to do something about the racial injustice in Mississippi – which is *still* one of the most racist states in the country – they didn't take the confederate battle flag off their state flag till 2021. Medgar Evers tried to do something about the segregation in his state. Joined the NAACP and started organizing boycotts. He helped investigate the murder of Emmett Till in Money, Mississippi. One morning, he comes home, carrying NAACP tee-shirts that read *Jim Crow Must Go*, and some KKK asshole was hiding in the bushes across the street. Shot him in the back with a rifle. Medgar managed to stagger to his porch. His wife was the one who found him."

Zahra could do nothing but shake her head. She felt sick to her stomach.

"You wanna hear some more fucked up shit about what happened to him?"

Zahra continued to shake her head. She didn't think it could get anymore fucked up than what he'd already told her.

"When they took him to the hospital," Demon said, "they wouldn't let him in 'cause they didn't treat black patients there. His wife had to tell them who he was and beg them for help. They let him in, but it didn't matter. He died an hour later – the first black man to be admitted to an all-white hospital in Mississippi.

"But it wasn't only Medgar Evers," Demon said. "The 16th Street Church bombing, Fred Hampton, a lot more names. Everything I learned taught me two things: They killing us, and we ain't killing them back, and whatever movement I wanted to start couldn't be public. The feds will come down on a nigga like flies on shit if you make a name for yourself. Plus, if I really was planning on going on a killing spree, staying under the radar was the only way to do that."

Zahra constantly found herself growing more impressed with this man. His rationale made way more sense than the manifesto she read a few days ago.

"So this group," she said, "you started it?"

He nodded. "The hardest part was finding likeminded individuals who were willing to join me. Do you know how hard it is to ask someone if they'll follow you down a path that leads to multiple murders, maybe even their own?"

Zahra had an idea. It took him nearly three months to trust her.

"I'ma tell you something else," he said. "Don't take this the wrong way, but while I was in Dallas checking up on you, I should've been in Georgia taking this white boy out. I think he's almost done with his manifesto, which means he might commit an attack at any moment. If that happens, I

75

won't regret my decision to focus my attention on bringing you in. At the end of the day, bringing in another soldier is more valuable than the casualties our people might incur in the process. But I will feel some kind of way about it."

Zahra's lips parted, but she had no response for that.

∞ ∞ ∞ ∞ ∞ ∞ ∞

They arrived at the airport and boarded their flight. Two and a half hours later, they landed in the Peach State. Zahra's stomach started to tighten the moment they touched down. After collecting their baggage, Demon led her to the rental car area, where he had a sedan reserved. The Toyota Corolla didn't seem like his style, but it was clean and fairly new. When they left the airport, Zahra thought he'd head to a hotel so they could unwind, maybe get something to eat. Instead, he drove to a self-storage facility deep in the city of Atlanta. Zahra was confused as he pulled up next to a keypad and entered a code that allowed them entry.

He navigated the facility as if he'd been there many times and pulled to a stop in the middle of the maze of storage units.

Before he exited the vehicle, he told Zahra, "I have a car in there. When I pull it out, can you park this one inside?"

"Uh, sure..." She did not question why they couldn't proceed in the car he just rented. By then she understood that everything he did was with purpose and planning.

She got out of the rental and made her way to the driver's side. She got behind the wheel and saw Demon backing out a black Charger that was more suitable to his dark persona. She wasn't able to swing the rental into the empty unit on the first try, but she eventually got it in there. Demon stood by patiently until she exited the car. She tossed him the keys, thinking he'd comment on her parking, but he remained mute. He transferred their bags from the trunk of the rental to the Charger before pulling down the rollup doors and affixing the lock. Five minutes later, they were back on the freeway.

He did take them to a hotel this time, but they didn't stay long. As he unloaded their bags, Zahra noticed another duffle bag that had been in the trunk already. She didn't inquire about it or have to wait long to find out what was inside. Inside their hotel room, he placed the new bag on the couch and unzipped it. He produced a gun case, placed it on the sofa and popped it open. Zahra didn't know much about guns, other than this one was large and black.

Demon expertly popped the magazine from the pistol and checked to make sure there wasn't a bullet in the chamber. He offered the gun to Zahra.

"Here."

She remained frozen in place. "What?"

"Take it."

Frowning, she said, "For what?"

His eyes narrowed. "Have you ever held a gun before?"

"Yes – maybe once or twice."

"This is a Glock 19," he said. "I need you to familiarize yourself with it. You may need it tomorrow."

As much as Zahra wanted to be done with their murder, she couldn't deny the relief that washed over her. "We're not doing it till tomorrow?"

He nodded. "I'm about to take you to a gun range. You won't be able to hear me that well when we get there, so

77

I need you to learn how to use this gun now. Here," he said, still offering the weapon.

She took it from him this time.

It took about five minutes for him to give her the basics of how to load, cock and shoot the gun. He showed her how to unchamber a round and eject an unused bullet from the chamber. He told her what to do if the gun jammed. When he was done, he gave her a simple two-question quiz.

"What makes the Glock 19 different from most other guns?"

"It doesn't have a manual safety," Zahra recalled. "Once you cock it, it's ready to shoot."

He nodded. "And what's the most important rule of gun safety?"

"Don't ever point a gun at something you don't want to shoot, even if you think it's unloaded."

By then, her stomach was in knots. She hoped he didn't notice her unease.

"Alright," he said, taking the weapon from her. "You ready."

Zahra felt like she was anything but.

Demon returned the gun to its case and hefted the bag. "You ready?"

"I – I need to go to the bathroom first."

He grinned. "You got the bubble guts, don't you?"

"Jesus," she said as she hurried past him. "You don't need to know *everything*."

∞ ∞ ∞ ∞ ∞ ∞ ∞

Zahra didn't completely suck at the gun range, but unless her real target was within six feet, she didn't think she'd be much help when the time came. She told Demon as much when they got back in the Charger.

He surprised her by saying, "You did fine."

"Um, no I didn't. All of your headshots hit the mark. *None* of your shots missed the target."

"Everyone in the group has something they're good at. The guys we got on the computers haven't touched a gun since they popped their cherry. We all have a role to play."

"What about you?" she asked. "What's your role?"

"I do pretty much everything. Recruitment. Reconnaissance. The murders."

Zahra remained self-conscious. "What if you don't find anything I'm good at?"

"You're down for the cause. That's good enough: A soldier who's tired of sitting back and letting them do us any kind of way. That alone makes you an asset to this group."

Zahra nodded, her heart hardened. "Okay. I trust you."

He chuckled. "Why you keep telling me that?"

"I don't know. Seems like every day I trust you more."

He watched her eyes for a few seconds before saying, "Good." Then, "You wanna get something to eat?"

"Damn. I thought you wasn't never gon' ask!"

He laughed at that.

∞ ∞ ∞ ∞ ∞ ∞ ∞

For dinner, he took her to The Busy Bee, arguably one of the best soul food restaurants in the city. The menu boasted their fried chicken was voted the best in Atlanta, so

Zahra went with that. It came smothered over rice. Demon ordered chicken and waffles. When the food came, Zahra was so ravenous, she didn't speak through much of the meal, other than to tell Demon how good it was. He felt the same way about his selection.

Towards the end of the meal, Zahra told him, "Thanks for bringing me here."

"You're welcome, but you don't have to thank me for feeding you. You're my responsibility. I'm gonna make sure you're taken care of."

Zahra was taken aback but also grateful to hear that. Other than her grandmother (and occasionally her mother), she couldn't recall anyone who ever considered her their *responsibility.*

She smiled as she said, "Tell me something embarrassing that happened when you were in school."

His eyes narrowed. "Of all the things you could've asked me, where'd that come from?"

She shrugged. "I don't know. You just seem so – *put together.* So bold and confident. I wanna hear about a time when you were vulnerable."

Still frowning, he said, "Why?"

"'Cause you almost don't seem like a regular person," she explained. "Have you ever slipped and busted your ass? Cut yourself while shaving?"

He smiled back at her. "You tripping. Ain't nobody perfect."

"You seem like you are – to me at least."

"Alright," he said. "Something real embarrassing happened to me in middle school. I think I was in the sixth grade. Back then, I was funny-looking."

Zahra smirked at him. "*Whatever.*"

"No, for real. I had to grow into my looks. I was what they call a *late bloomer*. None of the girls liked me in middle school, but I still had to shoot my shot. I wrote this girl a love letter. Her name was Crystal. It was stupid, one of those *Do you like me?*, with the *Yes* or *No* box."

She laughed. "You didn't put the *Maybe so?*"

"Yeah, I did," he said chuckling. "I told one of my friends to give it to Crystal, and she told one of her friends to give it back. Actually, three girls came with Tonya when she gave the note back to me. They were giggling, so I knew they all read it. Anyway, Crystal checked the *No* box, but she felt the need to further embarrass me by writing in an explanation. She wrote, '*No, cuz you ugly!*'"

Zahra's jaw dropped.

"Yup," Demon said. "Took me a while to live that down, especially since she let her friends read it, and they were all the prettiest girls at the school. If any of them was even *thinking* about liking me before that, they would never admit to it afterwards."

"Damn, that's cold."

"I got her back, though," Demon said.

"How'd you do that?"

"I told you I was a late bloomer. By the time I got to high school, I'd say my sophomore year, the girls wasn't calling me ugly anymore. They thought I was cute."

Zahra understood that. She felt the same way. Her smile was back now.

"I didn't know how to handle it at first," Demon said. "I was still going out with the girls nobody else wanted, but a pretty girl asked me out one time, and I knew something was different. Fast forward to my senior year, and guess who had eyes for me..."

81

"Crystal?"

He nodded. "I didn't want nothing to do with her. I remembered what she did to me, how it made me feel. Thinking back on it, I know what I did to her was wrong, but sometimes the underdog gotta get his revenge."

Zahra was all into this story. "What'd you do?"

"I went out with her. She was ready to give it up after three dates, so I planned for when we could make that happen, and we did it. After we had sex, I stopped taking her calls. She confronted me at school one day, and I had a note ready for her. I gave it to her and walked away."

Zahra had a good idea what was on the note.

He told her, "The note said, *'Do I like you, Yes or No?'* I checked the *No* box and wrote in, *'No, cuz you ugly!'"*

Her eyes widened. *"Oh, my God."*

"I know. I was wrong. I regret it, but I didn't feel bad about it back then. Guess you could say I had *revenge sex* before that was even a thing." He rolled his eyes in dismissal. "That's a story about something embarrassing that happened to me and also about how I was an asshole. I ain't as perfect as you thought, huh?"

"That was a long time ago. I know you're not the same person."

He shook his head. "No, I'm not. Now I'm something worse; *a demon.*"

Zahra had momentarily forgotten about their plans for tomorrow. Now the murder was front and center.

"I don't think you're a demon," she told him. "I think the people we're after are the ones who are evil."

"Don't get it twisted. There's nothing self-righteous about what we're doing. What they did – or are planning to do – is wrong, and what we're doing is wrong. Two wrongs don't make a right."

"I think there are levels to wrong," Zahra countered. "What we're doing is nowhere near as wrong as what they're doing – or what they're planning to do."

"I agree," Demon said. "They take one of mine, I feel obligated to take one of theirs. They done took so many, we got a lot of catching up to do."

Zahra thought that was a *huge* understatement.

∞ ∞ ∞ ∞ ∞ ∞ ∞

It was after eight when they got back to the hotel. Demon told her to try to get some rest; they'd head out first thing in the morning. Zahra got the lay of the suite when she went to take a shower. There was only one bedroom. After bathing, she dressed in a tank top with wind shorts. She left the room, in search of the man who considered her his responsibility. In the front room, Demon was seated at a small table, working on his laptop. He looked up at her, taking in her outfit, which wasn't necessarily *intimate*, but it was a more intimate view than he'd previously been provided.

He told her, "This sofa has a pullout bed. I'll sleep out here."

Zahra nodded. Though this was what she'd expected, she wouldn't say it was what she wanted.

"Not sure if I'll be able to sleep tonight," she told him.

"I get that. Maybe you can find something on TV you're interested in. If nothing else, it'll help pass the time."

"What about you? You gonna be working for a while?" She didn't know how to tell him that she didn't want

83

their time together to come to an end – didn't think it was appropriate to do so.

"Yeah, I'm checking on some people," he replied. "For every person we target, there's a hundred more on our radar. I gotta weed out the ones who are an immediate threat."

"Is there something I can help you with?"

"Not yet," he said, his eyes back on his computer. "You not ready. But I can train you. Don't worry. Pretty soon you'll have more than enough to do, probably more than you can keep up with."

Zahra accepted that and accepted that she was not going to get any more of his attention that day.

As she backed out of the room, he told her, "I'm gonna take a shower in a little bit. If you wanna close the bedroom door, you can. I'll knock before I come in, to make sure you're decent."

Zahra didn't plan to undress again, but she appreciated the courtesy. "Okay," she said and left him to his work.

CHAPTER SEVEN
OPIOID CRISIS

Zahra wasn't asleep when Demon appeared in the doorway the next morning. Her eyes were closed, but she didn't feel like she'd slept the whole night. She sat up when he knocked on the doorframe.

"Morning," he said. His voice strong and gruff. "We need to get going."

She stared at him as she nodded stiffly. He was fully dressed in jeans, sneakers and a tee-shirt, as was his norm.

He was past the point of asking if she was ready or if she was sure about what they were about to do. Although he hadn't revealed any information that could be traced back to his group, Zahra knew the group existed, and she knew his full name. She was always free to back out and go back to her old life, but as far as he was concerned, she'd become a liability if she chose to do so.

He told her, "You don't have to pack your things. We'll be back here later."

"Okay."

"I'ma brush my teeth and wash up." He entered the room and headed for the bathroom. "I'll only be a minute. When I'm done, I'll leave you alone to get ready."

∞ ∞ ∞ ∞ ∞ ∞ ∞

Zahra didn't think she rushed when he left the bathroom, but she got dressed in record time. She emerged from the bedroom and saw Demon sitting on the couch, perusing his phone. He looked up at her and then stood and hefted his black duffle bag.

"You ready?"

She nodded. "Yeah, I'm ready."

"You don't seem as shook as I thought you'd be," he said as they exited the suite.

Her mouth was so dry, she could barely get her response out. "Guess I'm doing a good job at hiding it."

"The first one's always the hardest," he assured her. "If you can get through what we're about to do, you can get through anything."

What if I can't get through this? she wondered but didn't say out loud.

They left the hotel with all the appearances of a vacationing couple. When they got in the Charger, Demon headed north.

As he drove, he told her, "John's Creek is thirty miles away. Won't take us long to get there."

Zahra swallowed. Nodded.

"I gotta make a stop in Peachtree Corners," he revealed. "I got a connect who's gonna let me steal his UPS truck."

Frowning, she said, "We need a UPS truck?"

"We got a bit of a disagreement in our group," he informed her. "Actually, it's a pretty big disagreement. I won't get into it now, but for the time being, we operate under a cloud of secrecy – I mean with the murders. We don't want the feds to get wise to us and start linking these killings together. I understand why that makes sense, but it also makes what I do a lot more difficult. So far, all of our murders have been different. I've set up everything from accidental drownings to freak electrocutions. Sometimes we'll just put a bullet in their heads, but even then, we'll make it look like a robbery."

Zahra thought she was in over her head when she woke up this morning. She couldn't begin to process her role in something like he was describing.

She asked him, "What are we gonna do with a UPS truck?"

"It's gonna get us in his house," Demon explained. "Everybody opens the door for UPS, even if they're not expecting anything. I'ma tell him I need a signature for a package. He's gonna open the door to see what the hell I'm talking about. Once he does that, I'm getting in his house," he said assuredly. "You're gonna wait about thirty seconds and then follow me inside."

Zahra's heart was racing again. She told him, "Okay." Frowning, she added, "Won't the police be looking for the truck?"

"Not right away," Demon explained. "My connect is gonna stop by his house during his lunch break and leave the truck outside. I already have a spare key for it. I'm gonna take off in it, with you following. I'll call our computer guys when I pull off. They're gonna disable the truck's tracker. My connect is gonna wait 45 minutes before he reports it stolen. By then, if everything goes well, we'll be done at the target's house, and the truck will be abandoned on the side of the road miles away."

Shaking her head, Zahra couldn't help but tell him, "This, this is too much."

"I agree," Demon said. "But this is how we do things in our group, and this is what's happening today. We have a one hundred percent success rate with all our killings. The police have never linked any of them together. I can't argue with success, even though I might do things differently, if it was up to me."

"I thought you started the group..."

"I did, but it's a democracy. We don't have an official leader. Me and Cujo are the closest to that, but everyone has a say in what goes on."

Zahra couldn't stop her mind from spinning. "Who is Cujo?"

"You'll meet him later. Right now, I need you to focus on the task at hand. When I take this truck, I need you to get behind the wheel of this car and follow me. We'll leave the Charger at a park. You'll get in the truck with me, and we'll go take care of business. You got that?"

There was nothing tricky about those instructions, but she still felt completely lost.

"Yeah. I got it."

"Good," he said, checking his phone. "We'll be there in ten minutes."

∞ ∞ ∞ ∞ ∞ ∞ ∞

In Peachtree Corners, Demon followed the GPS on his phone to a quaint neighborhood that was mostly quiet at

9am. Sure enough, when he turned on the last street of his destination, Zahra saw a big, brown UPS truck parked in front of a nice, two-story home. The scene was so commonplace, she half expected a driver to hop out and grab a package from the back. But Demon was sure that everything he had told her would unfold exactly as he said it would. He casually parked behind the truck and reminded Zahra to follow him when he pulled away.

He exited the Charger and walked to the back and opened the trunk. Zahra didn't see what he was up to until he closed the trunk and walked towards the truck. He had the black duffle bag with the guns inside. The door of the UPS vehicle was not locked. Demon climbed in with no problem at all, but then something happened.

Nothing happened.

Zahra waited.

After a couple of minutes, she was sure that something had gone wrong on his end. His spare key didn't work. Or maybe it fit the ignition, but the truck wouldn't start. After four minutes, she began to nibble her nails subconsciously. She looked around, noticing the traffic was light in the neighborhood, but it wasn't nonexistent. One of the cars she spotted drove down their street, right past them. None of the occupants paid attention to whatever Demon was doing or stared at the Charger parked behind the UPS vehicle, but Zahra couldn't take her eyes off them.

At the five-minute mark, her pulse had spiked. She debated whether she should get out to check on him, but then the truck's powerful engine cut through the silence of the neighborhood. She blew out a sigh as the truck's brake lights shone on the hood of the Charger, and the big, brown vehicle began to roll forward. She put the car in gear, her eyes as wide as saucers, and followed him.

Per his plan, Demon drove out of the neighborhood and into another one not far away. Zahra saw that they were indeed headed for a park, a large one. Thankfully it was completely deserted. Demon came to a stop in the parking lot. Zahra stopped behind him and waited a few beats before remembering that it was her turn to make the next move. She parked the Charger and locked the doors when she got out. She hurried to the passenger side of the truck and hopped inside. She was surprised to see Demon dressed in a complete UPS outfit.

"Where'd you get that?" she asked, her eyes dazzled as he put the truck in gear and got moving again.

"My partner left it for me," he explained.

At that moment, Zahra realized why it had taken him so long to drive away when he first entered the truck.

She shook her head in disbelief. "You felt like you had time to change right in front of his house?"

"That's the best place to do it. Everyone in the neighborhood knows he works for UPS and brings his truck home for lunch. On the other hand, a UPS truck sitting at this park for five minutes while I'm changing – *that* looks suspicious."

She agreed that it would.

"But if we come back to this neighborhood after he reports the truck stolen, won't the police be in the area?"

"I got another car stashed close to where we're leaving the truck. We'll hop in that, come back here to get the Charger, and leave the other car. That car's a throwaway. When they get around to towing it, they won't be able to trace it back to nobody."

Dammit if he didn't think of everything.

"I guess the next stop's our target," she breathed.

He nodded. "John's Creek is about ten minutes from here."

Zahra tensed. She sucked a deep breath through her nose and exhaled slowly.

"Alright. I'm ready."

He watched her for a moment before he shrugged. "Shit, I guess we'll see."

∞ ∞ ∞ ∞ ∞ ∞ ∞

When they pulled into the target's neighborhood, Zahra mentally went over her next instructions and realized they were inadequate. Demon said they'd arrive at the house in the UPS truck and use the subterfuge to gain entry into the home. Zahra had no doubt he'd be successful with that, especially with the UPS uniform he'd acquired. She was supposed to wait thirty seconds after he entered the home and then follow him inside.

And then what?

She assumed Demon would gain entry by sticking a gun in Eric Slater's face and ordering him back inside the house, but what was Zahra's role in the murder? Demon put a lot of effort into this sordid scheme. It was unlikely that it would end simply with a bullet in the head.

"You never said what I was supposed to do, once I get in there," she said as he came to a stop in front of a small, one-story home. Nothing about the place was remarkable. Even the Camry parked in the driveway was not the mode of transit she'd expected for the racist they were hunting.

Demon put the truck in park and killed the engine. "Just follow my lead. Hand me that bag."

Zahra hefted the bag he kept the guns in. Demon concealed one of his pistols in the small of his back and handed her the other.

"I don't know what that means," she said, cradling the weapon, "follow your lead...?"

"It'll make sense once we get inside. Remember, give me about half a minute before you follow me. I'll have everything set up for you. Free kill."

Free kill?

Noticing her confusion, he winked at her. "Let me get that box."

Zahra reached between her legs for a box she'd been trying to avoid stepping on since she entered the truck. She handed it to him, and he got out without another word. With the box in hand, he appeared to be an official deliveryman. He followed the walkway leading to the target's door as if he had every right to be there. The only thing off about him was the large pistol tucked in the small of his back, which was visible to Zahra, but the mark wouldn't see it until it was too late. She watched as he shifted the medium-size box to one hand and reached with the other to ring the doorbell. Her nerves had been stressed to the limit all morning. She now felt as if her overworked nervous system might simply give out on her.

How would Demon react if she never showed up for her appointment in thirty seconds, and he later found her passed out in the truck? Although everything that had happened since her grandmother was murdered followed a logical set of steps, actions and decisions, there was nothing normal about what she was doing and where she was. This was—

Someone opened the door.

Zahra quickly sat back in her seat, out of view of whoever had answered. From her vantage point, she could no longer see Demon. She felt like the hairs were standing on every inch of her body. She stared straight ahead. Listening to her own breaths. She swallowed and winced at the sensation it caused her. Her throat was so dry, it felt like she'd swallowed a fifty-cent piece. After thirty seconds that felt like a half an hour, she slowly inched forward until she could see the doorway again. This time it was empty. The door was closed. Demon had gained entry. She blew out a pent-up breath and waited. Another thirty seconds passed. Or maybe it was only ten. She doubted if it mattered. Demon was holding the man at gunpoint inside the home. She didn't think she'd be interrupting anything if she was a little early. He was waiting on her, after all, so she could pop her cherry.

Free kill.

She slid to the driver's side of the truck and left the vehicle on legs that felt like they'd atrophied. She remembered her gun a moment before she closed the door. She reached back for it and held it under her shirt, not sure how Demon expected her to conceal it. She closed the door and headed up the walkway, trying her best to appear casual. But there were so many things wrong about this. What if a neighbor spotted her getting out of the truck? She didn't have a UPS uniform. Surely, they would find this odd. On the porch she saw that the doorbell Demon had pushed was actually a *Ring* doorbell, equipped with a camera. She stared into the camera lens, her mouth ajar. Demon planned everything to the letter, but had he accounted for this? She forced herself to tear her eyes away from the camera.

The door was not fully closed. She pushed it open with no resistance. In the front room, she encountered the scene she'd expected. Demon stood holding his gun, his arm outstretched. Across from him, a white man cowered on the couch. He was dressed in boxers and a tee shirt. Zahra knew he was 22 years old, but he looked eighteen. His hair was a shaggy, brown mop. His terrified eyes moved from Demon to the new arrival. His shock gave way to a pleading expression. His chest rose and fell sporadically, much like Zahra's had while she waited in the UPS truck. His teeth rattled when he returned his attention to the man with the gun.

"Please. I didn't do anything. I don't, I don't, what, what's happening? Why are you doing this?" He held both hands up. All ten of his digits trembled.

Demon's demeanor was the exact opposite. He didn't look angry, anxious, or hurried. His voice was calm when he spoke. Deliberate.

"Alright," he told him. "Now that everyone's here, I'ma tell you what's going on."

"Please, man. Please don't do this."

"It's okay," Demon comforted him. "This is just a robbery. Nobody's gonna get hurt."

Slater's shock was replaced by confusion. "What? I don't – I don't have anything. I don't – I don't..."

"You *do* have something," Demon stated. "And if you don't, then we'll chalk this one up to a case of hitting the wrong house. But everybody got *something*. Maybe you don't think it's enough for us, but we'll be the judge of that."

"Okay, man. Okay. *Take whatever you want!*" His eyes moved to Zahra again. *"Please don't hurt me."*

"I'm glad you're being so reasonable," Demon said. "That'll make this a lot easier. Before we check out what you got back there, I'ma need you to take these pills." He reached into his pocket with his freehand. Zahra was just as surprised as the target when he produced a pill bottle.

The man's eyes bulged. *"What – what's that for? I don't want it. I don't wanna take that."*

"Baby, you got yo gun?" Demon asked.

Zahra was so caught up in the drama, she wasn't immediately sure that he was speaking to her. She locked eyes with him and then realized she wasn't playing her part. She exposed the gun she was holding under her shirt.

"Ye – yeah. I got it."

"Keep it on him, while I get him some water," Demon instructed.

Zahra trained her gun on Slater. He first watched her before focusing his attention on whatever Demon was doing. Zahra watched Demon too. The man in charge headed for the kitchen, which was in full view of the living room. He placed the pill bottle and his gun on the counter, speaking to Slater as he did so.

"I gotta give you these pills to put you to sleep." He reached into his back pocket and withdrew a pair of latex gloves. He took his time putting them on. "I don't want you calling the police on us as soon as we leave."

"I'm not gonna do that! I swear."

Slater rose halfway out of his seat. Zahra's heart was thunderous as she cocked her gun, just as she had done at the gun range. Just as Demon had taught her.

"*Don't move*," she growled with a resilience that belied her trepidation. She had no idea what Demon's plan was, but there was no denying they had the upper hand. Nothing would take place in that house unless they wanted it to.

Slater stared at her. Zahra could see him weighing his options. Would she really shoot him? If not, could he overpower her, take her gun, and swing it in Demon's direction in time to end this ordeal in the most ballsy way possible? For a moment, she thought he might try his luck. But he saw something in her eyes that made him sit back on the sofa. By then Demon had found a glass. He approached the sink and filled it with water. Nonchalantly, he returned to the counter and placed the glass next to his pistol. With his gloved hands, he opened the pill bottle and shook two pills into his palm. He returned to the living room with the pills and the water. Slater started shaking his head.

"I'm not taking that. I don't know what that is. I'm, I'm not."

"I told you, it's some sleeping pills," Demon said. "I ain't gon' lie, this some heavy shit. You'll be out in about ten minutes. When you wake up, we'll be gone. You can call the police and get your insurance to reimburse you for whatever we take. Trust me, this is the easiest way for this to go down."

"Trust you? *Why would I trust you*? I'm not taking it. I don't know what that is!"

Demon placed the water and the pills on the coffee table. Unperturbed, he returned to the kitchen and hefted his gun from the counter. He returned and said, "If you wanna go that route, that's fine. We'll just kill you and

96

bounce. You can keep all yo shit then, a lot of good it'll do you..."

Slater continued to shake his head. His eyes filled with tears. Those eyes. They reminded Zahra of a mouse she'd once caught on a glue trap at her grandmother's house. The poor thing was completely stuck, all four legs and its belly. Zahra could feel the terror emanating from the rodent as she approached the trap, knowing there was no way to dispose of it humanely. The mouse's beady eyes looked everywhere for one last ditch effort of escape, but there was none.

Slater was much smarter than that mouse. His beady eyes searched the souls of both of his intruders before settling on the water and the pills.

"It, they're just sleeping pills?"

"I ain't got no reason to lie to you," Demon replied. "I mean, what the fuck you think they are? If I wanted to kill you, I coulda did that shit when you opened the door. I ain't got no reason to hurt you. I don't even know you. I'm a burglar. I do home invasions. Might even snatch an old lady's purse if I get hungry enough, but I don't like to do no murders. I don't need that kind of heat."

He was so convincing, if Zahra had just met him, she would've believed everything he'd just said. Slater *had* just met him, and he was inclined to believe as well. He reached for the pills and the water. He swallowed the unknown narcotics and returned the glass to the table.

"Oh, okay. What now?"

"Open yo mouth," Demon ordered. "Let me see that you really swallowed 'em."

Slater did as he was told.

97

"Lift your tongue," Demon said, then, "pull yo gums down. Alright. Let me get you some more water."

He took the glass back to the kitchen and returned with it full again. He placed it on the table. Slater didn't have to be told what to do this time. He reached for the glass and didn't return it to the table until it was empty. He sat back on the couch.

"Alright. So, so now what?" he asked again.

"Now, we wait," Demon said.

"How long?"

Demon watched him closely. "I told you, about ten minutes."

"I just, I just sit here then."

Demon nodded. "Yeah. We all gon' hold our positions until it kicks in..."

It took only eight minutes for the pills to kick in, and when they did, Zahra knew that they weren't sleeping pills. Slater's eyes glazed over. His jaw went slack, and his head began to bob – or *nod*, as junkies would call it – as he tried to hold it up. Demon placed his gun on the coffee table and approached him. He moved him to a lying position, with his legs dangling off the couch. Unexpectedly, he stuck a finger in the man's nose. Zahra's mouth fell open, but then she understood what he was doing. The man did not react to the foreign object in his nostril. He made no move to brush it away. Demon stepped back and grinned at Zahra. Other than a sigh, she was unable to react.

"We gotta get moving," he said.

"What'd you give him?"

"OxyContin laced with Ambien. Our friend here has an addiction, 'bout to become another statistic of the opioid crisis."

"He's a drug addict?"

"No, but that's the way they're gonna write up his overdose. You know what they say; your first time might be your last time."

He removed a syringe from his front pocket along with a small vial. Zahra watched as he removed the cap from the syringe and expertly filled it with whatever concoction the vial contained. She'd encountered plenty of needles in her lifetime, for various reasons with different doctors. Until this moment, she had never seen a needle *completely* full. Demon placed it on the coffee table and reached into his pocket again. It seemed as if his pockets were bottomless pits of death and destruction. This time he produced a tourniquet. Zahra thought she was past the point of being surprised by anything he did, but there seemed to be no end to his resourcefulness. He applied the tourniquet around Slater's arm and reached into his back pocket for another pair of gloves. These he handed to Zahra.

"Here. Put these on."

Zahra understood what her role would be then. She did not shy away from it. She placed her gun on the table and pulled the gloves on, her breaths hot and steady now. While she did so, Demon reached for the man's arm and found the vein. He tapped it. Zahra saw that it bulged blue against his pale skin. By then, Slater was snoring lightly. Demon reached for the needle again and carefully inserted it in the man's arm. He barely had enough room to draw the plunger back, but he did, and the top of the syringe filled with blood that gradually mixed with the drugs in the needle. Holding the needle in place, he looked to Zahra.

"Alright. All you gotta do is push."

She stepped closer. At that moment, it occurred to her that she had not read the manifesto Slater was supposedly working on. Demon hadn't shown her any of his posts on 4chan or the websites of any of the hate groups Slater frequented. She was about to murder a man based solely on Demon's assertion that this man had to die.

She reached for the needle. She was closer to Demon than she had ever been. Close enough to feel his breath on the side of her face. Close enough to turn and kiss him. She thought of her grandmother. She thought about Medgar Evers. She thought of Clementa Pinkney and the other victims at Emanuel African Methodist Episcopal Church. She thought about what Gerald Lee Henry had to say about that mass murder.

That's how you do it. That's how you make a statement.

But mostly she thought about her grandmother. Her smile. How even though Granny usually woke up an hour before Zahra, she wouldn't drink her morning coffee until Zahra got up and made it for her, because she felt like, *"You make it special."*

She considered all of these things in less than five seconds, and then she pushed the plunger, all the way, probably faster than she should have. If so, Demon didn't complain. He withdrew the needle and the tourniquet, and they both backed away. Zahra watched, seemingly in a daze, as he took hold of Slater's hand and put his fingerprints on the needle, making sure to leave a fresh thumbprint on the plunger. He dropped the needle on the floor in front of the couch. Slater had not moved. Demon left him to gather his supplies. He used a handkerchief (what *didn't* those pockets have?) to wipe down the few surfaces he'd touched with his bare hands, before he had put on his gloves. By then Slater had begun to react from whatever was in the needle.

The man on the couch grew more pale, right before Zahra's eyes. His eyelids darkened, and his lips took on a bluish tone. Zahra thought they'd wait to make sure the deed was completely done, but Demon had no doubts. He headed for the door. Zahra was mesmerized by the overdose, but she grabbed her gun and followed him. She looked back when Slater began to emit a gurgling noise. She saw white foam and spittle bubbling at his lips.

He's going to choke to death.

She wondered if this would happen before the drugs in his system stopped his heart or if he would drown on his own vomit. Even though Demon put him to sleep before she pushed the plunger, Zahra knew this would be a messy, disgusting death. She wondered if Slater would begin to thrash about and fall to the floor, like the overdoses she'd seen on TV. Thanks to Demon's forethought and planning, her first murder seemed easy, but it was more foul than simply putting a bullet in his head.

Free kill.

"Come on," Demon said, drawing her attention away from the dying man.

He opened the door with his handkerchief and wiped the other side of the doorknob before stepping onto the porch. Once outside, he wiped the Ring doorbell as well. It was still mid-morning, but the sunlight was almost blinding when Zahra emerged from the house. Everything inside her, even her organs, seemed unsure of what to do next. The only thing that truly made sense was to follow Demon back to the truck.

So that's what she did.

CHAPTER EIGHT
IN THE DARK

Demon drove the UPS truck to another neighborhood, ten miles from Slater's home. Zahra didn't see anything special about the last street he turned on, other than the area was low income and at that hour, there was not a lot of pedestrian or vehicle traffic.

He told her, "Be ready to move fast. I'm gonna pull up next to an alley. I don't think we made any missteps with the truck, but if they *do* link it to the murder, they'll do forensic work on it. I gotta light this bitch up, the cab at least. Once I do, we gotta book it. Follow me down the alley. About halfway down, we'll jump a gate into a backyard. Our next ride is in the driveway of that house. Think you can make it over a gate?"

Zahra still felt numb. She was slow to respond. "What kind of gate?"

"Sorry, it's a fence. Regular old chain-link."

She nodded. "Yeah, I think so."

He frowned at her. "You alright?"

She nodded. "Yeah."

"It's okay if you a little shook. I would be, if I was in yo shoes."

She nodded again.

"Alright," Demon said. "Here comes that alley. Just head down the alley and wait for me. I won't be long."

He pulled the truck to a stop.

"Let me get that bag before you go."

Zahra handed it to him and hung around long enough to see him unzip it and remove a can of lighter fluid she didn't know was inside. Her door opened right in front of the alley, so she headed that way. Demon didn't bother wiping down anything inside the cab of the truck, but he did wipe the door handles on the driver and passenger sides before squirting so much lighter fluid inside, the can was nearly empty when he was done. He used the last of the lighter fluid to create a wet trail from the truck, down to the ground, leading towards the alley. The trail was almost ten feet long. He then tossed the empty can onto the passenger seat.

Standing next to Zahra, he removed a lighter from his pocket and told her, "Be ready. It's gon' hit like a small explosion. You should probably take a few more steps back..."

She heeded his warning and was glad she did. When he lit the trail, the fire raced towards the truck, and then the whole cabin went up with a *WHOMP!* that was both audible, searing, and explosive. If she had been standing any closer, Zahra guessed her eyelashes would've been singed. She may have lost them completely.

With his duffle bag gripped tightly in his hand, the two ran down the alleyway, which was not paved and mostly overgrown. He stopped at the backyard of one of the houses and helped Zahra over the fence. He handed her the duffle bag and then made his way over. Zahra's mind had been in a fog since they left Slater's home. Now it was in overdrive again. She followed Demon through the back yard to the other side of the fence. This time there was a gate, and it was unlocked. In the driveway of the home, she spotted a non-descript sedan that was backed in. Demon removed a key fob from his pocket and used it to unlock the doors.

Twenty seconds later they were rolling again. Though she was still awed by the totality of the man she was riding with, her growing misgivings about him were beginning to override all other emotions.

∞ ∞ ∞ ∞ ∞ ∞ ∞

They headed back to Peachtree Corners, where they'd left the black Charger at the park. Demon didn't speak to Zahra very much during the drive, but he made a few phone calls. He made no attempt to conceal his conversations, so Zahra didn't feel like she was eavesdropping as she listened in on them.

"It went off without a hitch," he told one person. "Yeah... I told him I had a package, and he opened right up. Damn near shit his pants when I stuck a gun in his face... Yeah, she right here with me now... She's fine, a little shook, but she's alright... Yes, she played her part..." He looked her way then. Zahra kept her eyes on the road. "No, I don't think so," Demon continued speaking into the phone. "... We didn't stick around long enough to see, but I know he outta there. Gave him damn near 50 units, the whole fucking needle. Fentanyl laced with heroin. Enough to kill a horse. Ain't no way he made it through that."

In another call, he asked someone, "You made sure to fix that doorbell, right?... Yeah, I know... I know, I'm just..." He chuckled. "Alright, man. You ain't never missed nothing before. Just made me feel funny staring at that camera... For real?" He looked Zahra's way again and told her, "The computer guy says you was staring at the doorbell camera for a long time, looked like you was finna take off running."

Seeing that she didn't find the humor in that, he told her, "It's alright, though. The feed from that camera goes into a computer, and you already know what we can do with *anything* that goes into a computer."

To the person on the phone, he said, "Can you book us a flight home?... Yeah, for today." He checked the time. It was a little after noon. "I gotta few things to do before we head to the airport, but we should be ready by six... Alright, bet."

When he hung up, he gave Zahra a look and asked, "You sure you okay?"

"Yeah. I told you, I'm good."

A few worry lines appeared on Demon's forehead, but he let it go for now.

∞ ∞ ∞ ∞ ∞ ∞ ∞

When they reached the park where they'd left the Charger, Demon took a couple of minutes to wipe down the sedan he was driving, but he told her it wasn't a necessity.

"This car's not stolen. No one's gonna dust an abandoned car for prints."

Zahra figured he was right about that.

From Peachtree Corners, he drove to the self-storage they first visited when they arrived in Georgia. He pulled up to the same unit as before and left the Charger to retrieve the rental car. Zahra did a better job parking the Charger in the empty unit this time around. Before he locked it up, Demon transferred his black duffle bag to the trunk of the Charger. At that point they were unarmed, so Zahra knew there wouldn't be any more dangerous surprises coming her way. Her expression remained deadpan, not revealing how much relief that brought her.

It was after one when they returned to the hotel. Upon entering, Zahra headed for the bedroom. Demon reached and took hold of her hand, turning her back towards him. They faced each other, him curious, her – not sure what to feel.

He broke the silence.

"At some point, you gon' have to talk to me – especially if you coming back to Texas with me."

At the mention of her home state, her heart fluttered. "You taking me home?"

"That wasn't my plan, but I can, if you want me to."

"What's in Texas? You told the person you were on the phone with that we were headed home."

"Our group's headquarters is in Texas – Houston. That's where we're headed. But, like I said, if you wanna go back to Overbrook Meadows instead..."

She shook her head.

"Well, if you still rolling with me," he said, "why ain't you talking to me?"

She shook her head, trying to organize her thoughts. There were a lot of things she wanted to tell him. All she could manage at the moment was, "You wrong."

His eyes narrowed. "I'm wrong?"

"Yes. I don't like how you did me. You coulda told me what was gonna happen in that house. You had everything planned, but you left me in the dark. I don't like that." She felt strong, getting it off her chest, but her eyes glazed over. Her emotions made her feel weak, which made her even more upset.

"I didn't leave you in the dark," Demon reasoned.

"You didn't tell me we were taking a UPS truck until we were about to do it."

"Okay, well, yeah, but I told you."

"I didn't know we were gonna burn it afterwards, and we had to take off running down some alley."

"Sometimes these jobs require us to run – and set shit on fire."

"But you didn't tell me."

"No, you right, I didn't."

He watched her. She was on the verge of tears, but he still saw the spitfire who had captured his attention at her grandmother's funeral.

"You had all that stuff in your pockets at that man's house. You knew exactly what you wanted to do to him. You coulda told me."

"It's not that simple."

Her hand was propped on her hip now, head cocked. "Why it ain't?"

"Because it was your first job, and it was a *complicated* job. You were freaked out enough already, just having to kill somebody. If I woulda threw all that heavy shit on you, you prolly woulda been too scared to get out of the truck."

107

Zahra couldn't outright deny that. She hadn't known about all the heavy shit, and she still almost didn't get out of the truck.

"It doesn't matter how you thought I was gonna react. You said it was my kill. That means I got a right to know everything about it."

"Okay. You right. I'm sorry."

She didn't respond, only sighed gruffly.

He grinned at her. "You know, you still cute when you mad."

She rolled her eyes at that.

"How long you gon' be mad at me?" he asked. "Till we get to the airport? All the way back to Texas?"

Her frown intensified.

"I'm just saying, it's gon' be a little weird introducing you to the group if you still mad at me when we get there."

"Why shouldn't I be mad, when you not even taking me seriously?"

"I am taking you seriously. I apologized, didn't I?"

"Yeah, and you over there smiling."

"I'm sorry." He chuckled and then caught himself. "Don't take that to mean I'm not taking you seriously. It's just the way you looking, like you mad enough to cut a nigga."

And he thinks I'm cute, Zahra thought, and couldn't help but grin herself.

"You forgive me?" he asked.

"Yeah, I guess so. Just don't do it again."

"I promise I won't."

She sighed and then said, "There's something else I was wondering about."

"What's that?"

"Don't you think it would've been better to tell Slater why we were killing him? It wouldn't have changed the outcome, but I think he should know why we were there. That should've been the last thought he had before he died."

"Actually, it *would* have changed the outcome," Demon countered. "If he knew he was about to die, he would've tried to make a run for it or fight us off. We would've had to shoot him, which wouldn't fit the narrative we planned. I agree with how you feel, though. If I had it my way, we'd tell all of 'em why we're sending them to hell."

Zahra didn't feel like her questioned had been fully answered, but she let it go for now.

"You should get some rest," he suggested. "You been through a lot this morning." He headed for the couch and plopped down on it. He checked his phone, and it immediately took most of his attention away from her. "Looks like our flight's earlier than I thought. We need to leave here in an hour, if we wanna stop and get something to eat on the way to the airport."

Zahra hadn't thought about food all day, but now that he brought it up, she realized she was ravenous.

"What you gon' be doing until then?" she asked.

He looked up at her. "Nothing. Sitting here, checking on stuff."

She hesitated, wanting him to invite her to chill on the couch with him and sensing that was something he would never do. Since her grandmother died, she had spent more time with Demon than any other man. Under normal circumstances, that might have meant something. But whatever their relationship was, it certainly wasn't romantic, even if he did think she was cute.

She retreated to the bedroom and packed her things. She then reclined on the bed and killed time with her own phone until it was time for them to leave.

∞ ∞ ∞ ∞ ∞ ∞ ∞

Zahra was in better spirits when they left the hotel. When they got to the car, Demon asked what her tastebuds were craving.

She told him, "Would it be weird if I wanted to go back to The Busy Bee?"

"Nah," he said smiling. "I *totally* understand that. But if you want more soul food, we should try a different place, experience more of what this city has to offer. There's another joint around here that's getting a lotta buzz."

He took her to Big Daddy's Kitchen. He was right about the popularity. It wasn't dinnertime, but the restaurant barely had room to seat them. The establishment wasn't fancy, on the outside or inside, but it made up for the ambiance with some of the best fried catfish Zahra had ever been blessed with. Her plate came with macaroni and southern green beans.

After a couple of bites, she told Demon, "Don't look at me funny, if I eat all of this."

"I won't, long as you don't look at me funny if I eat all mine. We'll probably have the itis, by the time we get to the airport."

"That's cool. Sleeping is about the only thing to do on a plane."

Later, they were on the road again, with enough time to check in the rental car and make their four o'clock flight.

While he drove, Zahra asked, "This headquarters in Houston, your whole group will be there?"

"I doubt it. We didn't call a group meeting. Some of them will be there. Cujo for sure. I know he wants to meet you. And our computer guys. They do most of their work at that house. I'm sure they'll be there. Maybe a few others."

"How do you know Cujo wants to meet me?"

"He wants to meet everybody I bring into the group. He act like he don't trust my judgement, even though I never recruited a bad apple."

Zahra sensed she'd be scrutinized by this stranger who carried a lot of weight in the group and bore the name of a rabid St. Bernard who murdered a few people and tormented a woman and her child in the Stephen King novel.

"Don't worry," Demon said, sensing her anxiety. "Everybody in the group is cool. I know they gon' like you."

"Oh yeah? How you know that?"

"You fishing for compliments, or do you really think you'll get rejected?"

She frowned. "No, I didn't mean—"

"They gon' like you because I like you. And if any of them got a problem with you, I'ma tell 'em to shut the fuck up and keep it moving. You know why I'd tell them that?"

Before she could respond, he said, "It's not only because I like you. It's because I know a soldier when I see one, and you're a soldier. What we did today, what *you* did, it ain't too many people out there ready to take a stand like that. Even if that boy wasn't about to do something horrible – I know he was, but even if he wasn't – silencing him shut down *everything*. We saved lives today – *black* lives. Don't ever forget that. What we do ain't all about revenge. It's about putting our stamp on the future. So, you ain't gotta

111

worry about nobody in my group. I told you I'ma take care of you, right?"

"Yes. You told me."

"And you trust me to do that...?"

She nodded.

"Even after what happened today?" he said. "You still trust me?"

"Yeah. I do."

"Then put yo mind at ease. Cujo can be an asshole sometimes, but I'm a *demon*. Remember that."

"You not a demon."

"You sure about that?"

She nodded. "I'm sure. Wouldn't be getting on the plane with you if I wasn't."

CHAPTER NINE
HEADQUARTERS

Eric Slater gagged forcibly and then rolled from his prone position on the couch. He landed between the sofa and the coffee table, encountering the carpeted floor with a loud *BOOMP*! He struggled to make it to all fours, his thin arms trembling from the exertion. He promptly vomited once he'd secured the position. From Zahra's vantage point near the front door, she saw that his vomit was bright red, the color of blood. She knew that it was blood. The stench of it, the smell of the totality of the dying man, singed her nostrils. She felt her own bile rising in the back of her throat as she watched him.

Slater's head slowly rose, and they made eye contact. Blood continued to dribble from his mouth. His skin was deathly pale, his eyes sunken in dark sockets. As he stared at her, his mouth moved. He was trying to tell her something, but his voice had the quality of someone speaking under water.

He moved then. First one arm, and then a leg, and then the other arm. He crawled towards her, haltingly, and deliberately as he picked up speed. Zahra's throat closed on a scream that was forcing its way up. She backed closer to the door. When her back encountered it, she reached behind her and fumbled blindly for the knob. She couldn't turn away from Slater. She kept her eyes on him, because she knew that if he reached her and touched her, she would surely die. She could not explain this rationale, just as she had no explanation for a man who looked dead and *should be* dead yet was not dead.

In fact, he rose to his feet, no more than ten paces from her, and began to lurch in her direction, his arms outstretched, his mouth still working to extract what was surely a curse. Eyes frantic, Zahra twisted the doorknob furiously, but it would not open. On the other side of the door, she heard the motor of the UPS truck as Demon slowly drove away.

He's leaving me!

Demon, please! Don't leave me!

She awakened with a terror-filled gasp. Eyes wide, breaths coming in quick pants, it took a few moments to realize she was not in Slater's living room. She was on a plane, exactly where she had been when she fell asleep. She looked to her left and saw Demon, who had not left her. On the contrary, he had promised to take care of her. As her eyes returned to their normal size, she saw that he was watching her.

He said, "You alright?"

She nodded. She wasn't sure if she was alright, but she told him, "Yeah. I, um..." She sighed. "I had a bad dream."

Demon continued to watch her as he nodded, and then he did something he had never done. He reached and took hold of her hand. It was a simple gesture. Zahra wasn't sure why it made her feel as good as it did.

"Was it about what happened today?" he asked.

She nodded, now feeling self-conscious about the tricks her subconscious had played on her.

But Demon told her, "It's alright. If you didn't have some kind of reaction, you wouldn't be human. I can't say it'll get better with time."

"You still have bad dreams?"

Before he had time to respond, she knew what his response would be.

He shook his head. "I keep trying to tell you I ain't human. Don't know why you don't wanna believe me."

She shook her head, grinning. "How long was I sleep? Are we almost there?"

"You weren't sleep that long. I think the pilot said we have about thirty more minutes."

"Okay," she said, resting back in her seat. "Now I don't wanna go back to sleep."

"You can, if you want. I'll protect you."

"You gon' protect me from my dreams?"

"Yup," he said with a straight face. "Move over for a second."

As cramped as their seats were, Zahra didn't know what he meant. But she gave him some room, and Demon raised the arm rest that divided them. He put an arm around her, which felt tons better than holding hands, and pulled her closer. She rested her head on his shoulder.

"That better?" he asked.

Zahra didn't know if she should tell him how good he made her feel, so she simply nodded and said, "Yeah."

She closed her eyes, enjoying the scent and closeness of him. Although she was mentally fatigued, she did not sleep again for the remainder of the flight. That was probably for the best.

∞ ∞ ∞ ∞ ∞ ∞ ∞

They touched down in Houston and headed for the airport parking this time. Zahra wasn't surprised when Demon led her to another Charger, this one dark red. She chuckled as he pressed the button on his keychain to unlock the doors.

"How many Chargers do you have?"

He told her, "A few."

"Is this the only kind of car you drive?" she asked as he placed their bags in the trunk.

He replied, "Never know when I gotta shake a spot – quick, fast, and in a hurry. I need something with some muscle under the hood."

After what she'd experienced that day, Zahra understood every bit of that.

He drove for thirty minutes before pulling into a quiet Harris County neighborhood that was actually in the city of Tomball, a suburb of Houston. The home was much nicer than she'd expected. It looked to be worth half a million dollars. There were no cars parked out front. Demon pulled into the half-circle driveway and came to a stop near the front door. Zahra thought she saw a light on in the front room, but other than that, the place looked deserted.

She told him, "I don't think anyone's home."

"There's people here," Demon assured her. "Their cars are parked in the garage and driveway in the back." He killed the engine.

Zahra shook her head in wonderment as she stared out of the passenger side window. "I didn't know y'all were living like this. This house is beautiful."

"I told you we have donors, on top of what the computer guys can do with them banks. We need a place like this. Big enough for all of us to meet, if we ever have to. Out of the way. Lowkey."

"This is lowkey?"

"It's more lowkey than the Black Panthers headquarters. Our neighbors have no idea what we're doing here. They see us from time to time, but none of them are nosey enough to ask exactly who lives here. You ever heard of hiding in plain sight?"

Zahra was familiar with the phrase. She nodded.

"Shit sounds too simple to work," Demon stated. "But you'd be surprised..."

They exited the car and gathered their things from the trunk. Once inside the home, Zahra's admiration of the place grew. But her immediate focus was the two people who came to greet them in the living room. One was a woman, the other male. The woman looked to be Zahra's age, maybe a few years older. She had fair skin like Zahra. She was all smiles as she approached them. The man was more reserved. Tall and dark, Zahra couldn't get a read on him. He hung back, staring at them, his attention on Demon's new recruit.

"*Demon*. Damn, nigga. I missed you!"

The woman stepped closer and threw both arms around him. Demon dropped the bags he was carrying and

117

returned the affection. Zahra was embarrassed about the pang of jealousy she felt as she watched them. Was this another one of Demon's recruits? Were they so close because they'd known each other for a while, or was there something more?

The woman backed away and stared at Zahra, still smiling. "*Zahra.* Girl, I heard a lot about you. Can't wait to hear about your day!"

"This is Tasha," Demon said.

"Oh, shit, I didn't even introduce myself," Tasha said. "Hey, girl! It's real nice to meet you!" She stuck out a hand. "I'm usually a hugger, but I don't know you like that, so I'm just gon' shake your hand for now."

Zahra couldn't help but smile as she shook her hand. She liked this woman. Tasha was energetic and bubbly. She didn't look like a killer, but Zahra knew that every member of Demon's group had to kill at least one person as an initiation. Tasha was curvaceous, whereas Zahra barely managed a B-cup bra. Tasha wasn't wearing makeup. Her hair was braided like Zahra's but pulled back in a ponytail.

"This is Cujo," Demon said, acknowledging the man who had moved closer.

Zahra looked his way, and Tasha stepped aside so he could greet her.

"Nice to meet you," the man said.

He offered his hand. Zahra shook it. She was still smiling, but Cujo was not. He stood a few inches higher than six feet. He looked to be about forty pounds heavier than Demon. Most of it was muscle. He was clean-shaven, his hair cut low. He didn't look as terrorizing as the rabid dog whose name he bore, but even in this cordial setting, he was menacing. His grip around her hand was not uncomfortable, but it was strong.

Zahra told him, "It's nice to meet you too."

He withdrew his hand and looked Demon's way. "Can I holler at you, before you get settled in?"

"Yeah," Demon said. He left his bags by the door and told Zahra, "I'll be back in a minute," before following Cujo out of the room.

When they were alone, Tasha took Zahra's hand and led her to the sofa. "Come sit down. Take a load off. I know you been ripping and running all day."

Zahra followed her to the sofa, her eyes on the hallway Demon had disappeared through.

Noticing her distraction, Tasha said, "Don't mind them. Cujo always be acting funny when Demon bring somebody new here."

Zahra sat next to her and said, "I don't think he likes me."

"He'll be alright," Tasha assured her. "Anyway, tell me how it went today. Did he suffer? Please tell me that asshole suffered. What he look like when y'all pulled a gun on him?"

Zahra was surprised by the line of questioning.

"I know it was probably hard for you, since it was your first time," Tasha said. "But for us, this is a *good day*! Every time we get one of them racist motherfuckers off the street, it's a time to celebrate. I got some champagne in the kitchen. I woulda popped it open for you, but I didn't wanna take you too fast, have you thinking we a bunch of weirdos."

Zahra laughed at that. "Y'all celebrate?"

"Hell yeah, girl. But we don't have to do that today. I know how I felt when Demon first brought me to this house.

You probably think this is all a little too much to digest all at once." Her smile went away when she said, "I'm real sorry about what happened to your grandmother. The one who did that wasn't even on our radar. That's why I'm always happy when we get some more help. We so far behind, and it's so many of them."

Zahra nodded, not only thinking of her grandmother, but also the way Slater had appeared in her dream. She wouldn't say that she hated Slater at the moment they killed him, but she had no regrets about what she and Demon did to him. "He was scared to death when we had our guns on him," she told Tasha. "Sitting there in his tee-shirt and draws, he really believed we would let him live if he took those pills. When we hit him with the needle, it hit him hard. We didn't stay long enough to watch the whole thing, but I saw him foaming at the mouth. I'm sure he choked to death."

"Good," Tasha said. "He deserve every bit of that. All of 'em do. If it makes you feel better, you can tell yourself that was for your grandmama. He ain't the one who pulled the trigger, but they all the same. They all think the same."

Zahra sighed. That made perfect sense. After a moment, she asked, "Where'd you meet Demon? Did he recruit you?"

Tasha's smile returned. Zahra noticed how she lit up at the mention of his name.

"You remember when those cops got shot at a rally in Dallas?" she asked. "It was in 2016, after Alton Sterling and Philando Castile were murdered. Micah Johnson shot twelve police, killed five."

Zahra remembered that shooting. She recalled how shocking it was to have something like that happen so close to home. She remembered her grandmother telling her, "Foolishness like that make it hard for the people that was out there trying to make a change. You think them white folks gon' listen to them now? Nope. Ain't nobody gon' talk about what they was fighting for. They was trying to shine a light on bad police. Now everybody feel sorry for the police."

"I remember that," Zahra said.

"Last year, when that boy got shot in Pittsburg," Tasha continued, "I was on Twitter arguing with some white folks about racists cops. Somebody brought up what happened in Dallas, as if that was an excuse for what they doing to us. I didn't know much about Micah's shooting at the time, but I looked it up and got back on Twitter, *and I went in*. I was on there talking reckless for a couple of weeks. I got into arguments with a lot more people. Got my account suspended too, for saying Micah didn't kill enough police that night."

Zahra's eyes widened. Tasha didn't seem like that type of person at all.

"I know," she said grinning. "That shit was dumb, but one good thing came out of it. A couple of weeks later, some dude walked up to me when I was leaving the nail shop. He said he'd seen the stuff I was saying on Twitter. At first, I thought he wanted smoke. I was wondering how he found me, since my Twitter name wasn't even my real name. But he said he wasn't mad at me. He said he understood how I felt, but I was going about it all wrong. He said if I wanted to make a *real* difference, he could help me. He told me his name was *Demon*. I been rocking with him ever since."

When she was done speaking, all Zahra could respond was, "Wow." She admired Tasha's fortitude and the lengths at which Demon went to recruit members to the group.

121

Down the hallway, in one of the bedrooms, Demon faced much less admiration. He made sure to close the door before he confronted Cujo.

"That was rude."

"Rude? How was I rude?" Cujo had a deep voice that boomed even when he wasn't speaking loudly. "I told her it was nice to meet her and shook her hand."

Demon shook his head. The men faced each other, standing no more than five feet apart.

"The look on your face said everything. It don't matter what came out of your mouth, which was pretty much nothing. You saw the way Tasha greeted her. What you did was nothing like that."

"Me and Tasha ain't the same. And I already told you I don't think she was properly vetted."

"Well, I'm the one who vetted her, so I think I should be the one to decide that. Plus, she did her thang today. I told you how it went."

"Just because she got through one mission doesn't mean it's safe to bring her here. You know what's at stake."

"You don't think Head got enough intel on her? You know how diligent he is."

"I didn't say that."

"Speaking of Head, didn't you have this same reaction when I brought him in? You said he was a *nerd*, and we need *soldiers*. You remember that?" Before he could respond, Demon added, "Now look at him. We wouldn't be able to do half the shit we do without him and Einstein – another nigga *I* brought in."

"Don't make it sound like you doing all this on your own. I brought in just as many people as you."

The look Demon gave him made Cujo retract that statement.

"Okay, not as many as you, but I do my part. We all do."

"And I don't give you half as much shit as you give me." Despite their size difference, Demon didn't give up an inch of space or audacity. "Either give me a reason why you don't trust her, a *real* reason, or keep your negativity to yourself. And I don't wanna hear about how you got a *bad feeling*."

"Since when don't it matter when I got a bad feeling about something? You weren't talking like this when my bad feeling saved your ass in New York."

"I ain't saying you're never right when you say that," Demon conceded. "But you not right about Zahra."

"You sure about that?"

It was impossible for Demon to be completely sure about any new recruit, but he told him, "Yeah. I'm sure."

"Alright. I'll leave it alone then."

"Thanks. I'd appreciate that."

∞ ∞ ∞ ∞ ∞ ∞ ∞

Cujo wasn't remarkably friendlier when the men returned to the front room, but he had more than a few words to say to Zahra. He offered condolences for her grandmother and asked if she was tired or wanted something to eat. She acknowledged her fatigue but told him, "We already ate dinner, but thanks for asking."

The four of them then moved further into the house, and Zahra had a chance to check out how spacious and well-designed it was. It looked like the home of a large, upper middle-class family, rather than the *headquarters* for a murderous group of militants who were trying to make up for hundreds of years of oppression, lynchings, and mass murders. The master bedroom had been converted into something that looked like a computer lab. There was no bed in the room, only desks and high-tech equipment, some of which Zahra recognized. Some she didn't.

She marveled at how organized and innovative everything was. All of the computers had double-monitor setups. There were maps on the walls, bookshelves filled with well-worn titles. Sitting at adjacent desks were two men who looked so *normal*, they didn't fit the picture of the brains of this operation that Zahra had in mind. But she knew these were in fact the *computer guys* Demon had been referring to. These were the men who had accessed her bank account, credit score, and provided enough vital information about her for Demon to purchase plane tickets and put her on a visitor's list at Huntsville penitentiary. They both left their work to greet the newcomer.

"Hey, how's it going," the first one said. He was tall with a small frame. He wore glasses and had a short afro that was mostly nappy. "It's good to see you in person. I've only had your pictures to go by." He studied her features. "You look a lot better than on your driver's license."

"Oh – thank you."

"I'm Einstein," the other man said. He shook her hand. "I watched you earlier today on that Ring doorbell. I'm glad you're here. Welcome aboard." Einstein was short and stocky. He wasn't big enough to have played college football, but Zahra could imagine him wrecking the field when he was in high school.

She told him, "Thank you. It's good to meet you."

Both of the men appeared to be in their late twenties.

"These are the guys I've been telling you about," Demon said. "When I tell you they can do anything with those computers..."

"We can't do *anything*," the first one said. "Some of those military databases are very secure."

"He's lying," the one named Einstein said. "He *can* do anything. I'm pretty good, but he puts me to shame."

"I didn't get your name," Zahra said to the first one.

"Oh, I'm Head. That's what they call me. I didn't pick that name. *He* did." He nodded towards Demon.

"I called him that 'cause of how smart he is," Demon explained. "It ain't got nothing to do with his big-ass head."

"But the fact that I do have a big-ass head made it sting a little," Head said to Zahra. "It's cool though. I'm over it now. Kinda like the name."

Zahra's smile was genuine. With the exception of Cujo, everyone in the group seemed like nice people.

"What y'all working on?" Cujo asked them.

"Same old, same old," Einstein said. "Got a few more targets ready for y'all." He returned to his computer. Cujo went to look over his shoulder.

"What about that militia?" Cujo asked.

"Got some good intel on them too," Einstein said, "but I think that's gonna be a no-go."

Cujo wanted to know, "Why?"

Demon answered for him. "Because that group is too big. We're trying to stay under the radar, and you wanna take out twenty men. We can't get 'em all at once without every cop in the state investigating it, and they'll be on to us if we take 'em out one-by-one."

"They not that damn smart," Cujo retorted. "Even if they are, if we want the most bang for our buck, we should do something about them. They gearing up for a race war. The people we taking out got it coming too, but our fight is bigger than that. It's time to start going after the soldiers."

"If we get caught, it's gon' be a war for real," Demon countered. "Not just with the militias, but with the feds too. We ain't got the numbers to take any of them on. Now, if you wanna try it *my* way, and start leaving calling cards, we could go after that militia tomorrow."

Cujo blew off that idea. "Man, that's dead in the water."

Zahra couldn't pick a side as she listened to the back and forth. She didn't understand enough about either of the men's plans to have an opinion. Even if she did, this was her first day at the headquarters, so she still would've remained mute.

After a few minutes, the conversation had gotten nowhere, and Demon shut it down.

"We can talk about this later. It's been a long day. I'ma go get some of my things unpacked." He asked the rest of the group, "Y'all gon' be here for a while?"

"I'm almost done with what I'm working on," Head said. "I was just hanging around to meet Zahra."

"Me too," Einstein chimed in.

"I know it's late, but I was thinking about making some spaghetti," Tasha said. "I'll make enough for everybody, if y'all wanna eat before you go."

The computer guys said they wouldn't mind some home cooking.

Demon headed for the hallway. He looked back and locked eyes with Zahra, "You coming?"

"Yeah, I'm going with you." Before following him out of the room, she told her new acquaintances, "It was nice meeting y'all." To Tasha: "I might try some of your spaghetti, see what you working with."

"You should," Tasha said. "But if you decide to turn in for the night, I'll see you tomorrow."

CHAPTER TEN
CORNERSTONE

Demon returned to the front room and hefted their bags before leading her upstairs. Zahra counted four more bedrooms up there, with another living room in the middle.

He took her bags to one of the bedrooms and told her, "The restroom's right outside your door. I'll be in the room on the other side."

Zahra looked over the space where she'd spend the night. The bed was large, a king-size. The sheets and blankets were freshly laundered. There was a desk in one corner, a large TV mounted on the wall, and more bookshelves. She knew Demon did a lot of reading on his phone, but it was clear that this group took their literature seriously.

"Do you spend the night here a lot?" she asked him.

He nodded. "Unlike most of the others, if I'm not sleeping in a hotel somewhere, this is where I call home. Some of the others sleep here too, on and off, depending on what they got going on."

"It sounded like none of them are staying tonight."

"I know Tasha isn't," Demon said. "She got a boyfriend in Houston. She usually spends the night with him."

That revelation flooded Zahra with a warm sense of relief. She fought the urge to smile.

"Head got *several* girlfriends," Demon continued. "Ain't no telling where he'll go when he leaves here."

Zahra couldn't hide her reaction to that.

Demon chuckled. "Don't let his nerdy look fool you. That nigga be laying pipe."

Zahra laughed.

"Einstein got his own apartment," Demon went on. "He *could* live here, but he say it's too big to be here all alone, if everyone else leaves. Plus, he likes his privacy."

Zahra understood that.

"And Cujo, he's married with two kids. He moved them from Cali to Houston when he joined the group. He don't never spend the night here. I'm the only one who got nowhere to go when I'm not doing a mission."

"Not anymore," Zahra said. "I got nowhere to go, either."

"I hope that doesn't make you feel some kind of way."

"No. Not really. I feel like I lost my home when my grandmama got killed. I was homeless before I joined this group."

Demon watched her for a moment and then asked, "You wanna talk about it – your grandmother?"

She shook her head. "No. I don't wanna cry right now."

"I get that, but how are you doing? I know you hurting..."

"I am. When she got killed, I felt like I was lost. Didn't know what was gonna happen. But you gave me a reason to move on. I know it sounds corny, but you gave me a *purpose*."

He was quiet for a few seconds before saying, "I don't think that's corny. If you're not living your life with some kind of purpose, I think you're wasting your time. I wish more of our people felt that way. If you need anything or you change your mind about wanting to talk, I'll be right over here. Depression can set in fast, if you start feeling lonely."

She told him, "Okay, thank you." Looking around the room, she asked, "Are we gonna be here for a while? Should I unpack?"

"You can. I'll make sure everyone knows this is your room from now on. But we'll probably be on the road again soon, maybe tomorrow."

"Alright."

He offered a comforting smile before backing out of the room.

∞ ∞ ∞ ∞ ∞ ∞ ∞

Lured by the smell of home cooking and the sound of togetherness, Zahra left the room forty minutes later. Downstairs, she found everyone in the kitchen, Demon included. He was seated at the table, reading a book, rather than eating with the others. The crew was dispersed throughout the kitchen. Einstein and Cujo sat at the bar with a steaming plate of spaghetti before them. Head was seated with Demon. Tasha stood next to the stove, with her plate on the counter.

"Hey, Zahra," she said. "You changed your mind about eating?"

"Maybe. I just came to see what was going on down here."

"You said you might try some," Tasha reminded her and promptly began to fix another plate.

"Okay, but not that much."

"It's good," Head told her.

"Yeah, my wife is gonna be mad when I get home and tell her I'm not hungry," Cujo added.

Zahra accepted her plate and told her, "Thank you."

"Have you been thinking about what nickname you want?" Tasha asked.

"No. I forgot that everyone has a nickname. What about you? How come you don't?"

"I do," Tasha said grinning. "My real name is *Keisha*."

Zahra found that amusing. "And you chose *Tasha* as your nickname?"

"She didn't want a nickname," Demon recalled. "But it's important to have one, in case we have to call out to each other during a mission. Last thing we wanna do is say your real name and have a witness remember it."

"Not that we ever have witnesses," Cujo interjected.

"So far, no, we haven't," Demon agreed.

"I'ma come up with a name for you," Tasha said. She looked her up and down. "Can't think of one right off top, but I'ma come up with something."

Zahra took her plate to the table and sat with Demon and Head. He looked up at her and smiled before returning his attention to the pages of his book.

"What you reading?" she asked him.

He showed her the cover. "It's about the civil war. Have you ever heard of the Cornerstone Speech?"

She shook her head.

Demon flipped through the pages with such familiarity, she knew he had read the speech many times. He looked to the other person at the table and said, "Head, tell her why this speech is so important."

Head was quick to respond. "It's important because you got a lot of white folks, some ignorant black folks too, who are trying to rewrite history. Trying to say the civil war wasn't about slavery."

"When you meet someone like that," Demon cut in, "you should be ready to argue with them based on the *facts*. They can argue with their emotions all they want, but they can't argue with history. They can't argue with what's written in black and white." He tapped the page in his book.

Head jumped in. "The Cornerstone Speech was given by Alexander H. Stephens. He was the vice president of the confederacy. In the speech he clearly stated—"

Demon cut him off. "No, let her read it for herself. That's another problem with the way we get our information. We're always willing to let someone tell us something we should research on our own."

Tasha grinned as she approached the table. "There he go again. Demon always down for a history lesson. Girl, don't let him stress you."

"No, she needs to know this stuff," Cujo said.

Zahra felt like everyone in the room was watching her when Demon handed her the book, pointing to a particular paragraph.

"Read that," he said. "Read it out loud."

"Why you putting her on the spot?" Tasha said.

"It's alright," Zahra said. "Y'all got me interested now." Looking at the book, she asked Demon, "Where do I start?'"

"Right there where I was pointing. Where it says 'Our new government...'"

"Okay," Zahra said and started reading. "Our new government is founded upon exactly the opposite idea–"

"He's talking about the confederacy," Demon interjected.

"I think she got that," Tasha said.

"I'm just making sure she knows the context," Demon said. "The confederate government is founded on this part you're about to read. Alright, go ahead..."

Zahra started over. "Our new government is founded upon exactly the opposite idea; its foundations are laid, its corner-stone rests–"

"The *cornerstone!*" Demon was animated.

Tasha laughed at him. "Are you gon' let her read?"

"But that's the most important part," Demon stressed. "The *cornerstone* of their new government. The definition of cornerstone is *an important quality or feature on which a particular thing depends or is based.*"

Zahra stared at him in amazement. He was like a walking encyclopedia.

"Alright," he said. "Keep reading. Start from the top. Just those first two sentences."

She started again. "Our new government is founded upon exactly the opposite idea; its foundations are laid, its *corner-stone* rests, upon the great truth that the negro is not equal to the white man; that slavery subordination to the superior race is his natural and normal condition." She paused there. Not because Demon had stopped her, but

133

because she had never seen the fundamental principle of the confederacy laid out so plainly. "This," she continued, "our new government, is the first, in the history of the world, based upon this great physical, philosophical, and moral truth."

"That's it," Demon said, leaning forward with his elbows on the table. "So you can't never let nobody tell you the civil war wasn't about slavery and the confederate flag isn't racist. One of the founding fathers of the confederacy done already told the truth, and there ain't no changing that. If anyone tries to tell you the war was about *states' rights*, what would you tell them, Head?"

"I'd say yeah it was, the southern states' *right to own slaves*."

Demon sat back in his seat, satisfied with the answer. "Damn right."

And there it was again, that awe Zahra felt for this man. Not only was he skilled, organized, resourceful and determined, but Demon was also a teacher. He had told her there was no official leader of their group, but it was clear that everyone in the room looked to him for guidance.

"I want you to keep that book," he told her. "You should read the whole thing, but you can start with that speech. Most of it's boring, legislative stuff. But the ideology in that speech is the same ideology we're up against now."

"Okay," Zahra said. "I'll read it. I'll try to read the whole book."

"Take your time. You got plenty time."

"And plenty more books you should check out," Cujo added.

Zahra suddenly felt as if she'd be letting them down, if she didn't grow to become as smart as them. She took a deep breath and nodded, her eyes back on the Cornerstone speech.

∞ ∞ ∞ ∞ ∞ ∞ ∞

Zahra took a long, hot bath that night. She usually didn't sleep in anything but a tee-shirt and panties, so that was all she had to put on when she stepped out of the tub. The door to Demon's room was closed when she entered the bathroom. Not knowing if he'd opened it since then, she wrapped a towel around her lower half before exiting. His door was still closed, but the light shining under the door let her know he was still awake.

It was after eleven when she climbed into bed with her phone and the civil war book Demon had given her. Normally her phone would've stolen her attention from a book, but the small portion of the Cornerstone speech she had read had her intrigued. Ten minutes later, she had finished reading the speech. She agreed with Demon's assertion that it was mostly about boring, legislative matters. But the parts about slavery and the confederate's view of black people was both repulsive and compelling. She flipped back to the first chapter, intent on reading the whole book in the next few days.

She didn't hear Demon leave his room, but he poked his head in after a while.

"I see you're still up – and you're reading," he noticed.

"I finished the speech," she told him. "Figured I'd read the rest of the book."

"What do you think about it so far?"

"It's interesting. All I know about the Civil War is what was in the history books at school."

135

"That's about to be less and less," Demon said. "Did you hear the Texas Board of Education is considering a proposal to call slavery *involuntary relocation?*"

Zahra shook her head in wonderment.

"Not sure if it'll go through," Demon said. "But the fact that it was even proposed says a lot. These white folks are doing whatever they can to avoid their children dealing with *uncomfortable* history lessons in school. I wanna go to one of those board meetings and ask them how comfortable they think it was for slaves to get whipped, raped, and lynched. None of this shit that's going on today is about *our* comfort – never has been."

Zahra nodded, listening, learning from him.

"I'ma take my bath," he told her. "You need anything?"

"No. I'm good."

"Okay. Let me know if you change your mind."

An hour later, she was done reading for the night, but she wasn't sleepy. She was restless. She went to the bathroom and saw that Demon's light was off this time, his door closed. Before leaving the bathroom, she stared at herself in the mirror. She never considered herself a beauty queen, but at that moment she questioned whether she was pretty at all. None of the men she'd encountered recently had done or said anything that made her feel pretty. She supposed that was appropriate, considering the nature of the group and comrade relationship they shared.

But still.

The only person she would've welcomed a compliment from was Demon, but he treated her like she was just one of the guys.

She left the bathroom and turned off the light in her bedroom before crawling into bed.

Thirty minutes later, her eyes were still wide, even though she hadn't been on her phone. She left the bed again and looked through her suitcase in the darkness. When she found what she was looking for, she left her room again, walking quietly, her heart thudding slowly and powerfully. She walked to Demon's room, raised a hand to knock on his door, and then withdrew her hand. She stood there, wavering in indecision, for an unknown amount of time. She gathered her courage and raised her hand again. This time she knocked.

His response was immediate. "I'm still up. You can come in."

She tried to swallow down her insecurities as she turned the knob and pushed the door open. Demon was in bed, lying on his back, on his phone. With the light from his phone, she could see his face clearly. But he could not see her.

He asked, "Is something wrong?"

"No," she said. "Not really. Just – I don't know."

"You lonely in there by yourself?"

Her face flushed with heat. "Yeah."

"I can't see you," he said. "Turn on the light."

She almost told him she didn't want to do that. He might not like what he saw. He might be offended. She gathered the same courage it took to knock on his door, and then she reached and flipped on the light.

Demon's eyes adjusted quickly to the brightness. He saw more of her than he ever had. More than he wanted to? She was dressed minimally, in a tee shirt that was short enough to reveal the bottom of her panties. He looked her up and down, taking in her eyes, legs, her uncertainty and vulnerability.

She told him, "I'm sorry. I can leave, if you want me to."

It took him so long to respond, she felt like she might die while waiting.

He told her, "I don't want you to leave. But you can turn the light off, if it's making you uncomfortable."

She turned the light off and remained frozen in place. He placed his phone face down on the bed, and the room was almost completely dark.

He asked her, "Do you want to get in bed with me?"

"Yes. Is that okay."

"It is, but—"

She had taken a step forward. Now she was frozen again.

"I need you to know that I have never laid in bed with anyone from our group," he finished.

Although that was something she wanted to hear, she asked him, "Does that mean you don't want me in your bed?"

"No. I'm not saying that. But the reason I haven't is important. It could complicate things. Our group doesn't have an official leader, but we do have structure and levels of authority. With you being new, I'm kinda like your boss. You're dependent on me. You're a subordinate."

"Do you think I'm pretty?"

"What, I..."

She didn't have to see his expression to know the question caught him off guard.

"Zahra, I think you're beautiful. You're a strong, confident, black queen. I think you're sexy. I love your eyes, the way you look at me. Your lips. I always thought you were fine, but seeing you tonight, with that tee shirt... You're everything any man would ever want."

His words soothed the very core of her being.

"I don't feel very confident right now. I never do, when I'm around you."

"I'm sorry you feel that way – sorry if I've done something to make you feel that way." After a few beats, he said, "After all I've said, if you still want to get in bed with me, come on."

"Do you want me to? Not because you feel sorry for me or because you don't want me to be lonely. Do you want me to come because you want to be with me, and you saw that I have a condom in my hand?"

Demon had seen the condom when she turned the lights on.

He told her, "Yes, I want you to come."

∞ ∞ ∞ ∞ ∞ ∞ ∞

Their lovemaking was more encompassing, more fervent and fulfilling than anything Zahra could've expected. Demon was an attentive lover. His hands were warm and curious, exploring every inch of her. Her hands were equally eager, as was her soft lips and hot, hungry tongue. They did not speak as they tasted and caressed and pleased each other in the darkness. When he entered her, Zahra sucked air between her teeth. Behind her eyelids, the room was bathed in sweet tones of jasmine, sepia and mint.

The only word that was spoken that night was when she came. She called his name then – not the name everyone in his current life knew him by, but the name his mother had given him, the name she had only used once since she'd known him. With her knees raised, her thighs pressed against him, his chest close to hers, and her breath on his ear, she clung to him when he released a torrent of ecstasy that felt like a thunderstorm rolling from her head down to her clitoris.

"David," she breathed. *"David."*

He grunted, and she felt his dick grow even harder, and then it began to pulsate deep inside her. The sensual sensation ushered another climax for Zahra, even though the first had not yet subsided.

"Dav – *Ooh, David...*"

CHAPTER ELEVEN
THE BROTHERS

The next morning, Demon was the first to rise. Zahra was awakened by the sound of him washing up in the bathroom. He returned to the bedroom wearing only his boxers and found her sitting up, her soft eyes still dreamy.

She'd done nothing to perfect her appearance for the day, but he asked her, "How you wake up looking so good?"

That put a smile on her face.

"I know you tripping," she responded.

"No, I'm serious." He approached the bed and leaned in for a brief kiss.

Zahra's eyes were even more lovestruck when he backed away, and then she thought she heard a sound downstairs.

"Is somebody here?" she asked him.

Demon nodded. "Yeah. Pretty sure that's Einstein. He said he was bringing breakfast."

"What time is it?" she asked, looking for her phone.

"A little after nine."

Demon walked to his closet and returned with a pair of jeans. As he stepped into them, Zahra asked, "Is he coming up here? Does he know we slept in the same room?"

"He shouldn't come up here. And it's not his business what bed we slept in."

Zahra wondered if that meant that what happened last night would be their little secret. She didn't ask. She pulled the sheets away and sat up on the side of the bed. Demon pulled his pants up and stared at her nude physique.

"What?" she said.

"Nothing. Can't a man look at a naked woman?"

"The door's open," she noticed. She reached back for the sheets and covered herself. "I know you said he's not coming up here..."

"I'm about to go downstairs. I'll make sure no one comes up while you're getting dressed. You can take your time."

"Okay. Thanks."

By then, he had pulled a tee shirt and socks from his dresser. Within a couple of minutes, he was fully dressed. Zahra smiled wistfully as she watched him.

"What am I doing that's got you so entertained?" he wondered.

"Nothing," she said. "I guess I like watching you as much as you like watching me."

"I get that."

He approached her again and bent for another kiss. This time he cupped the side of her breast as their lips touched. It was a simple gesture, but it sent a pulse of energy down to her clit. He backed away and headed out of the room. Before he disappeared, she called out to him.

"David."

He turned back to her. "Yeah?"

Once again, she considered asking if the group would know what happened between them last night. What she really wondered was if it meant something to him, or if it was just a one-time thing. She realized that was such a *woman* thing to ask.

She told him, "Never mind."

His eyes narrowed. "You sure?"

"Yeah. I'll be down in a minute."

"Okay," he said and continued on his way.

∞ ∞ ∞ ∞ ∞ ∞ ∞

Downstairs, Zahra found the living room and kitchen deserted. She saw a few large boxes from Taco Cabana on the counter. The thought of what was inside made her mouth water, but she headed for the voices she heard further down the hallway. In the master bedroom, Demon and Einstein were chowing down on breakfast tacos. Demon sat on a futon near Einstein's desk. Einstein was on his computer, already working. He turned to greet her.

"Morning. How was your first night?"

Zahra smiled and blushed. Due to her fair skin, she was almost certain he noticed.

"It was fine."

"What are your thoughts about us, overall?" he wondered. "I know we can be a strange bunch."

"I don't think that. I like all of y'all. You seem to get along with each other, and you're all so smart."

"You didn't want breakfast?" Demon asked her. "It's some tacos in there."

"Yeah, I think I'll go get some. Do we have coffee?"

"We have a Keurig," Einstein said.

"If you're making some, can you bring me a cup?" Demon asked.

She nodded. "Sure. How do you take it?"

"One Splenda with a little cream."

"You want coffee too?" she asked Einstein.

"Already got mine." He nodded to a cup on his desk. "But thanks."

Back in the kitchen, Zahra had to look through a few cabinets before she found everything she needed, but it didn't take long. Whoever took the time to organize the space had done a good job. She returned with Demon's coffee first and then went back for hers. By then, the men were discussing two brothers who had the misfortune of making it to the top of Demon's to-do list. Zahra didn't catch much of what they were saying, only that this mission felt personal to Demon.

"What they did is too much like what happened to my uncle," he told Einstein. "I hate that we live in a country where white folks think they got a green light to do something like that."

While she ate, the men went over the logistics of their next mission. Zahra wished she could contribute to the conversation, but she had no intel or insight. Demon didn't let her sit idly by for long. When he noticed she was done eating, he went to one of the bookshelves and returned with a paperback.

"You should read this."

Zahra accepted the book and told him, "I haven't even made a dent in the first book you gave me."

Einstein found that amusing. "Just be happy he's not giving you a quiz afterwards."

"Who said there wouldn't be a quiz?" Demon asked.

He gave Zahra a smile and a wink, but she wasn't sure if that meant there wouldn't really be a quiz when she was done. The new book was titled *I Am a Revolutionary: Fred Hampton Speaks*. She dove in and was fully enthralled for the next hour, as more members of the group arrived. Head came first, followed shortly by a man Zahra hadn't met. In his late forties, he was the oldest member that Zahra knew of. He had a bald head and a full beard that had yet to see a gray hair. He wasn't African, but he introduced himself as *Zulu*.

"It's real good to meet you," he said. "I'm glad you decided to join."

"Thank you. It's good to be here."

"What's that you reading?" he asked.

She showed him the cover. "It's a collection of Fred Hampton speeches."

"That's a good book. Demon turned you on to that?" Zulu had small eyes that glistened as he smiled at her.

"Yes, apparently I should be reading a book a day," she joked.

"Zahra gon' turn on him after a while," Head guessed. "Nobody wants you to give them a new book every day."

"Not Zahra, it's *Cleo*," Demon said. "Short for *Cleopatra*. That's the name she go by now."

That was news to Zahra. She was not opposed to him choosing for her or the name he picked. She didn't know much about Cleopatra, other than her being an Egyptian queen who was known for her beauty.

"Cleo, huh?" Zulu studied her features. "That fits you. Welcome aboard, Cleo."

145

Zahra glanced at Demon as she returned to her seat. He gave her an approving nod, as if she'd picked the name herself.

Cujo was next to arrive. Zahra felt a little uneasy at the sight of him. It didn't take long to realize this feeling was warranted.

After greeting everyone, he too inquired about Zahra's book.

"What you know about Fred Hampton?"

"Um, other than that movie about him, not much."

"Which movie?"

"The one that came out a couple years ago – *Judas and the Black Messiah.*"

"You like that movie?"

Not everyone in the room paid attention to their interaction, but Demon's focus was squarely on the two of them.

"Yeah. I thought it was a good movie. I didn't like the way it ended. It was messed up what they did to him."

"Fred Hampton was a revolutionary," Cujo informed her. "Watching a movie about him doesn't make you a revolutionary."

Zahra bristled. "I never said it did."

Cujo laughed it off. "I'm just kidding. That's a good book you got there. And that was a good movie. An important movie for our culture."

Even though Cujo tried to soften his remarks towards the end of their conversation, it took Zahra a few minutes to calm her nerves. She was happy when Tasha walked into the room, as fresh and bubbly as ever.

"Morning! What y'all got going on in here?" Her eyes lit up when she spotted Zulu. "*Zulu!* Damn, nigga, where you been?" She walked to him and gave him a big hug.

"I been around," Zulu said when they separated. "Demon called me in today, said y'all needed help with those brothers."

"Same thing he told me," Tasha said. "Glad we going after them." She locked eyes with Zahra. "Hey, girl. You already ate? Somebody brought tacos."

"That was me," Einstein said.

"I ate already," Zahra told her.

"I'ma go get me some," Tasha announced.

"I'll go with you." Zahra rose to her feet. "I think I want some more coffee."

Demon waited until the ladies were out of earshot, but not for a moment of privacy, before he told Cujo, "I thought you said you weren't gonna give Zahra a hard time."

"It's *Cleo,*" Einstein reminded him.

Demon ignored him.

"*Cleo?*" Cujo said. "I guess that'll work."

Demon continued to stare at him, waiting for a response to his comment.

"I didn't give her a hard time," Cujo said. "I told her I was just kidding."

Head swiveled in his chair to face them. "I wasn't gon' say nothing, but I thought you was kinda rude."

"I give all the new people a hard time," Cujo said. "It's like my little initiation. If they can't put up with me for a few days, ain't no way they gon' make it through what we got going on."

Demon didn't let him off the hook. "She don't need to be initiated. She already in the group."

147

Cujo frowned and then his eyes widened. "You fucking her, ain't you?"

The room became completely silent. All eyes were a little larger now, focused on Demon, who said, "That's none of your business."

Cujo's feature's softened as he smiled. "I guess that answers my question. I think the problem is even though I treat everybody the same, you taking it personally with this new one because you like her. I guess that's understandable. I'm sorry if I offended you or her. I didn't mean no harm."

Demon was so surprised by the apology, it took him a moment to respond. "Alright, thank you."

"Just do me a favor," Cujo said. "Don't let your feelings about her interfere with any decisions you make for the group."

"I would never do that."

"I'd like to think you wouldn't, but this has never come up before. We're in uncharted territory."

Demon couldn't dispute that, but he was confident the group's interests would supersede his feelings for Zahra. "That's not something you have to worry about." He was speaking to Cujo, but the assurance was for everyone in the room.

∞ ∞ ∞ ∞ ∞ ∞ ∞

In the kitchen, Zahra found it easy and enjoyable to talk to Tasha. It felt as if they'd known each other for years.

"He just *gave* you a name?" Tasha asked around a chorizo taco.

Zahra chuckled. "Yeah."

"That's just like Demon."

"I heard he gave a few of you your names."

"That's true. Not me, though. I came up with *Tasha* all by myself."

"I bet you were up all night trying to come up with that," Zahra said sarcastically.

"Actually, *I was*. That's why I gave up and told them to just call me *Tasha*. Couldn't think of nothing else that fit me."

"You said Demon called you in today, to help with this job?"

Tasha nodded. "I think he said we need five or six people."

"This is for the brothers?"

Tasha continued to nod.

"Did he say if he was using me?" Zahra wondered. "I don't know anything about it."

"I'm sure he'll fill you in, but I'll tell you what I know. These white boys, they live in West Virginia. They're blood brothers. They come from a long line of racists. Their father and a couple of uncles are locked up. They've all joined Aryan gangs in prison. The brothers been arrested a bunch of times, mostly for white trash shit – bar fights and DUIs. But neither one of 'em got a felony. Einstein been checking on 'em. They both bought an assault rifle in the past couple of months. They live in a trailer park. I think their trailers are right next to each other. We looked up their address on Google Maps and saw a confederate flag posted out front.

"The reason they hit our radar is because they killed a black man during a road rage incident about a year ago. We don't know exactly what happened, because we only got the white boy's side of the story. What we know for sure is they got into it with another driver one night, on one of them county roads close to where they live. The brothers pulled their pickup over, and the black man pulled over too. They exchanged words, and the brothers beat him to death. They didn't use no weapons, just punching and stomping. They left him there to die. Called the police when they got home and said he swung on them first, claiming self-defense."

Zahra's heart sank deep in her chest. She'd never heard about this incident. Now she understood why Demon had said the climate in this country made the brothers feel like they had a green light to commit a brutal act against a black man. She also understood why the murder impacted him on a personal level. His uncle was killed after a bar fight with a group of racist white men. The man who murdered him had told Zahra, "The day a black man thinks he can rise up and raise his hand to a white man is the day that black man has to be put down, like any dog that would bite its master."

"The brothers are currently on trial for the murder," Tasha continued. "Somehow, they made bail and have been on the streets. They show up for court every day and go back home to their trailer park. The lawyers are expected to give their closing remarks tomorrow morning, and then it goes to the jury. The brothers been popping off on the internet, talking about something big is gonna go down if they get convicted."

Zahra's mouth fell open. "They're saying that on Twitter?"

"Naw, on one of them underground message boards. Cujo and Demon have been going back and forth about this one."

No surprise there, Zahra thought, but she asked, "Why?"

"Cujo thinks taking them out is too risky, for a couple reasons: First, they're from *Gilmer County*. That's one of the poorest and whitest counties in West Virginia. There's no way a bunch of black faces can show up there and not get noticed. And if we *do* manage to pull it off, he thinks everyone will know it was a hit. A lot of people are watching this trial. Black folks think it was a modern-day lynching. The white nationalists are hoping for an acquittal. They see the brothers as heroes.

"Demon thinks we have to do this for the same reason. If they get acquitted, they'll gain more notoriety, like George Zimmerman. If they go to prison, they still win. They'll join prison gangs, like their daddy. They'll continue to have influence. They'll be treated like white knights."

Zahra thought Demon's assertion was correct. She didn't believe she felt that way because of the way she felt about him.

"They're being tried at the Northern District Court in Clarksburg," Tasha said. "That county is heavy on the mayonnaise too, but it's a lot bigger than Gilmer. Demon thinks we can get them there when they're coming from or going to court."

"*Heavy on the mayonnaise?*"

"Girl, you know what I mean. A lot of white folks."

Zahra would've laughed at that, if this conversation wasn't so serious.

"I don't know how he plans to pull it off," Tasha concluded. "But I know that whenever Demon decides it's time to make a move, he got everything planned perfectly. I trust him. What you think?"

"I'm with you. I know he'll make sure it works."

"You basing that on the one job you did with him, or you saying that 'cause you like him?"

Startled, Zahra asked, "How you know I like him?"

"Girl, it don't take no psychic to see that. You damn near had a fit when I hugged him yesterday."

"What? No, I didn't."

Tasha laughed at her. "I'm just kidding – about the fit, not about you liking him. Ain't nothing wrong with that. He like you too. I don't know if he told you yet..."

Zahra thought about the way he expressed his affection last night, and her face grew warm.

"Oh yeah, he done told you!" Tasha said grinning. "From the looks of it, he done *showed* you too. Come on, let's get back in there and see what these mens is talking about."

"Okay," Zahra said and followed her back to the computer room.

CHAPTER TWELVE
STAND YOUR GROUND

The ladies made it back to the computer room in time to catch the tail end of another disagreement that was going Demon's way. Cujo was offering his last-minute concerns, in an attempt to get the whole plan scrapped.

"This is the most complicated mission you've ever come up with," he surmised. "And you wanna use that Mexican to drive the truck... With so much at stake, why would you give the most important part of the job to him?"

"We've used him before," Demon countered. "He's never let us down."

"But he's not a part of our group."

"Maybe not officially, but he's fully committed."

The other three men in the room sat and watched the back and forth. Zahra and Tasha entered the room quietly and unobtrusively found a seat.

"He's down for the cause," Demon added.

"Down for the cause doesn't mean he's *part* of the cause," Cujo countered. "What you think he'll do if he gets caught?"

"The same thing any of us would do. He'll keep his mouth shut and wait for his lawyer. I know you don't trust him, but sometimes we gotta reach out for help. You need to accept the fact that no matter how many people we have, it's not enough."

"Alright." In a show of frustration, Cujo threw up his hands. "I see I'm not getting anywhere with this. Did you even ask the group if they cool with this job, or did you volunteer them?"

"You can ask them right now," Demon suggested.

Cujo sighed in exasperation. "What's the point. I know they not gon' defy you, while you're sitting here looking at them."

"Everybody in this room has a say. I'll always go along with the majority opinion. There's six of us here. If four don't think it's a good idea, we can let it go."

Cujo looked around at the anxious faces watching them. Knowing he wouldn't get the votes he needed, he said, "What about everybody who ain't here? Don't they have a say?"

"Listen, man. If you wanna give 'em all a call, do what you gotta do. But for something official like that, you should've told them to come this morning, so we could do it the right way. The Baker brothers go back to court tomorrow. No telling how long the jury will deliberate after the closing remarks. If they come back quick, the Bakers will be taken into custody immediately, and we'll lose our chance. You got a right to question my plan, but if it's going down, then we need to get moving. I got a lot of pieces to put together before tomorrow morning."

"Alright," Cujo conceded. "Your plan is a go. I back you one hundred percent. But can I ask a few more questions, just to make sure you got your bases covered?"

"Of course. Shoot."

"Do you know where the Bakers are right now?"

Einstein answered for him. "They're home, at the trailer park. Both of their cellphones are pinging off the usual tower."

"If you're planning to stage an *accident*," Cujo said, "don't you need to know the route they'll take to the courthouse tomorrow?"

"I know the most direct route," Demon said. "I can't say what roads they'll take in Gilmer, but when they get to Clarksburg, there ain't too many options. Plus, we'll be tailing them. I got that taken care of."

"What if they ain't alone tomorrow morning?" Cujo asked. "What if they decide to bring their girlfriends or maybe one of their kids with them?"

"Collateral damage," Demon said. He spoke so coldly, Zahra felt as if the temperature in the room dropped ten degrees.

"*Collateral damage*? We ain't never killed no kids before," Cujo said. "That's all you got to say about it?"

"Since when are *they* not okay with collateral damage?" Demon argued. "When they bombed the 16th Street Baptist Church, weren't those four little girls *collateral damage*? Don't ask me to take the high road when they walking into churches and grocery stores with assault rifles, shooting every black face they see. You can miss me with that. If one of 'em bring his son with them, so be it. The little bastard would probably grow up to be just like his daddy anyway. Might as well kill him now."

155

Even though Zahra knew this side of Demon existed, his words chilled her to the core. Everyone in the group knew they were fighting a common foe, but she didn't think any of them had fully morphed their enemy into one face as succinctly as Demon had. For him, there was no difference between the man who had killed her grandmother, the one who assassinated Medgar Evers, or the brothers who beat a black motorist to death on the side of the road. For Demon, they all had one ideology and one face. And there was but one way to rid the world of them.

"I hope it doesn't come to that," Cujo commented. "But it's your call. After this, I want you to put the same effort into the militia I've been talking about. You keep saying there's no way to pull it off. But if you can pull off your plan for tomorrow, you can do anything, and you know it."

Demon knew he was being bribed, but it was only fair that he gave Cujo's plan as much consideration as Cujo had given his. "Alright. I'll look into it."

Cujo checked the time on his phone. "What time y'all leaving?"

"As soon as possible." Demon asked Head, "Can you book the flights?"

"Yessir," Head said, swiveling his chair back to his computer. "All of y'all on the same plane?"

"That's fine," Demon said. "But book 'em separately – me and Cleo together and then Tasha and Zulu."

"Bet."

"And reserve three rentals."

"Under whose names?"

"One for me, the others for Tasha and Zulu."

"Got it. I'm on it."

∞ ∞ ∞ ∞ ∞ ∞ ∞

Upstairs, Zahra's heart was drumming with the same anxiety mixed with dread that she felt on the morning of Slater's murder. That felt like a very long time ago. In reality, only 24 hours had passed since she sat in a Charger parked behind a UPS truck Demon was commandeering.

He headed for his bedroom and told her, "Pack light. Try to get everything you need in your carry-on. We don't have time to wait for luggage after the plane lands."

Zahra nodded, willing and ready to follow his orders, like a true soldier. "How long will we be gone?"

"Should be back tomorrow. You only need one change of clothes."

"Does it matter what I wear?"

He shook his head. "If everything goes like I'm hoping it will, no one will see you. All you have to do is ride. I'll explain more later."

Zahra accepted that. She went to her room and stuffed the few things she thought she'd need into a backpack.

An hour later they were headed to the airport again. This time there were four of them in the car. Zulu rode shotgun, with Zahra and Tasha in the back. Zahra felt like she was the only one in the dark about Demon's illustrious plan, but Zulu and Tasha were also unaware of their roles. Demon provided more details as he drove.

"When we get to Georgia, we gotta drive about nine hours to West Virginia."

Zahra was surprised by that. "Why are we going back to Georgia?"

"Georgia is our tactical point for the east," Demon informed her. "We have another set up in Nevada, for missions on the west coast. Houston is our central headquarters."

"But why can't we fly straight to West Virginia?"

"Because we can't fly with all our guns and cars." Demon was patient with her, not condescending. "For everything on the east, we stop in Georgia to get what we need. You've been to one of our storage units. You know what we got in the trunk of those cars. We're planning to establish another tactical point in Florida and New York – one in Cali too. If we had more manpower, it would've been done by now."

Zahra nodded, girding herself for the flight and the nine-hour drive.

"You all know the trial is gonna end tomorrow morning," Demon continued. "The Baker brothers have been driving to court every day. Like I told Cujo, I'm not exactly sure of their route. But I know we can intersect them before they make it to the courthouse. We'll have a team tailing them and another in front. When they get to Clarksburg, they're gonna get T-boned by an eighteen-wheeler. It's gonna be a bad accident. A fatality incident. The chance of anyone in their truck surviving is virtually zero percent."

The car was silent as everyone absorbed this. Zahra didn't think she was the only one who had questions, but everyone remained mute.

"The Mexican Cujo is so worried about will be driving the 18-wheeler," Demon said.

"That the one who helped us in Arkansas?" Zulu asked.

Demon nodded. "That's him."

"I trust that man," Zulu said. "He's solid."

"I'll admit some of the logistics are iffy," Demon acknowledged. "But I think I've planned for all contingencies. Tasha and Cleo..." He looked up at them in the rearview mirror, "you two will be together. Next to the 18-wheeler, y'all got the most important role."

"And what's that?" Tasha asked.

"A diversion. Once we get the brothers to the right intersection, you'll box them in from the front."

"I'll be behind them?" Zulu guessed.

Demon nodded.

"What about you?" Tasha asked.

"I'ma scoop up the truck driver, make sure he make it outta there okay."

"How he gon' make it outta there if he crashing his truck into the Bakers?" Tasha wondered. "If it go down like you say, won't he get killed too."

Zahra thought that was a valid point.

Demon said, "I'm still working on that."

If any of them thought it was odd that he was still trying to figure out one of the most crucial parts of his plan this late in the game, they didn't speak on it.

Instead, Zahra said, "The Bakers, how are they even on the street, after what they did?"

Demon's eyes darkened. "I'm with you on that, but the case ain't as cut and dry as it seems – at least not from a legal perspective. How much do you know about it?"

"Just that they beat a black man to death after a road rage incident."

"His name was *Jaylen Campbell*," Demon said, his nostrils flaring. "Forty-six years old. Had three kids, two

159

grandbabies. They did him worst than you would do a mangy dog. Wasn't no witnesses. No red-light cameras on that stretch of road. Barely any streetlights. They claim Jaylen was driving too slow on the one-lane road, and they tried to pass him. According to *them*, he started driving aggressively, swerving to the other lane, so they couldn't pass. They kept this up for a couple of miles before they managed to get by him. When the Bakers got in front, they say he started tailgating them with his high beams on. They got pissed and pulled over, *supposedly* so he could pass them and go on about his business. But Jaylen pulled over too.

"According to them, he got out of his car first and took a swing at one of the brothers through the driver's window. No one knows if any of that shit is true. What we know for sure is one of the brothers had a scrape on the side of his face, and when the dust settled, Jaylen was lying dead in the middle of the road. Multiple contusions and broken bones in his face. Broken rib. A few teeth knocked out. Lacerated liver. When the police got the brothers down to the station, they still had blood on their boots. They knuckles was all bruised from beating on that man."

Zahra took a deep breath and blew it out slowly. Her breath was hot. She felt like the whole car was.

"They claimed self-defense," Demon reported. "Said Jaylen was the aggressor. One of 'em had the scrape on his cheek to prove it. My thinking is even if he did swing first, that don't give them the right to kill 'em. Not like they did. It was two against one. Problem is West Virginia is a stand-your-ground state. By law, they didn't have to back down from a fight. They said they kept punching and kicking him because he was still being aggressive. Of course, I don't buy none of that. I think they planned to kill that man the moment he pulled over. If he did throw the first punch, that just gave them an excuse.

"Anyway, it took the D.A. five months to charge 'em with the murder. That didn't happen until after a public outcry, once people looked into them boys and found out they was both racists. The murder made a lot more sense then, but it's still not open-and-shut. The way I see it, they got a 50/50 chance of being acquitted. That's why we gotta take care of this tomorrow. It rarely works out in our favor, when we leave it up to a jury. As far as their bail, they got a lot of white people supporting them. My guess is an anonymous donor bonded them out."

Zahra didn't think she'd ever met anyone who was always right – about everything. Why did Cujo bother arguing with this man? Everything Demon said made perfect sense.

As if reading her mind, he said, "Cleo, you need to look up this case and do your own research before we get there. Don't never let someone tell you how you should feel about something – not even if it's me."

Zahra thought that was one of the most unpretentious things he had ever told her. She pulled up Google on her phone and searched the name Jaylen Campbell.

Demon didn't speak much for the remainder of the ride to the airport. He did a lot of texting and made one phone call. He didn't have a lot to say to the man on the other end of the line, but he referred to him as *Sergio*. They had only spoken of one Mexican in the group, so Zahra knew this was the man who would play the key role in Demon's plan; bringing death and destruction to the Bakers by way of a 25 ton 18-wheeler. Her mouth was dry as she eavesdropped on the conversation.

CHAPTER THIRTEEN
HASHTAGS

Their plane touched down in Georgia at 2:30. After picking up their rental, they booked it to the same self-storage as before and swapped the Focus for the Charger. They stopped and got lunch from a drive thru before hitting the freeway again, this time headed for West Virginia. Zahra checked her GPS and saw that it was indeed a nine-hour drive. After eating, she settled in for the ride. She didn't mind the long hours on the road. And as much as she enjoyed Tasha's company, she was glad it was just her and Demon in the car this time.

He finished his lunch and made a few phone calls, first checking on Tasha and Zulu, who would have to make the trip alone in separate vehicles. They had both swapped their rentals and were on the freeway, headed in the same direction as Demon. He then called Sergio again. From Zahra's perspective, Sergio's preparation wasn't going as well as Demon would've liked.

"What do you mean late?" he said. "How late you talking?... You know court starts at 8:30. They've been on time every day. The way I see it, they'll be at the interception point at 8:15... Sergio, this has got to be *precise*. If you're one minute early or one minute late, the whole thing will fall through. You got the truck yet?" Demon rubbed his forehead and sighed in exasperation. "Alright. If that's the way you wanna do it, I'ma let you handle it. But I think that's cutting it too close... Okay... Alright, I'll holler at you later."

When he disconnected, Zahra asked him, "Is everything okay?"

"Yeah, I think so. So many moving pieces. Cujo was right about this being one of the most complicated plans I've come up with."

"Do we have a Plan B, if Sergio doesn't come through with the truck?"

"Yeah, we could just pull up alongside the Bakers and shoot 'em. Not much of a plan, though. We don't have a safe place to run to in West Virginia. With so many witnesses, it's doubtful we'll be able to flee the scene and make it all the way back to Georgia."

Zahra agreed with that assertion.

They drove in silence for a while. Zahra was glad she'd brought both of her books. She was about a third of the way through the collection of Fred Hampton speeches. She read a few more pages before Demon asked her, "Why do you think I do what I do?"

She looked over at him. "Because of your uncle."

"That's part of it."

"To stop white supremacists from committing mass murders?"

"That's part of it too. But my grievance is with an ideology that goes way, way back, before the days of James

Byrd and George Floyd and all the hashtags you've heard about. Back in the 50s and 60s, most of our martyrs barely got a mention in the newspaper. No protests or rallies, just dead black people who are now gone and forgotten." To prove his point, he asked her, "Have you ever heard of Herbert Lee?"

Zahra shook her head.

"He worked with civil rights leaders in Liberty, Mississippi in 1961, trying to register black people to vote. Herbert was killed by a white state legislature. Can you believe that? The man claimed self-defense and never even got arrested. Another black man who witnessed the murder ended up getting killed too, for trying to tell people what he saw."

Zahra frowned at that.

"What about Willie Edwards Jr.? Ever heard of him?"

She didn't know if she should feel embarrassed by responding, "No."

"Montgomery Alabama, 1957," Demon said. "A truck driver, minding his own business, got stopped by four members of the KKK. They mistook him for another black man who they said was dating a white woman. They held him at gunpoint and forced him to jump off a bridge into the Alabama River. They didn't find his body for three months.

"In 1962," he continued, "Corporal Roman Duckworth Jr. was on leave. He was a military police officer, stationed in Maryland. He traveled to Mississippi, because his wife was expecting their sixth child. During one of the stops, a white cop ordered him off the bus, thinking he was a freedom rider. Roman argued with the cop and ended up getting shot dead. The cop was never charged. If that wasn't bad enough, somebody lit a cross on fire outside of his house while his family was grieving. Forced them to move. Tell me how that makes sense."

Zahra didn't have a response. Demon didn't wait for one.

"I know you know about Emmett Till," he said, "but what about Virgil Lamar Ware?"

Zahra felt sick to her stomach. Her subconscious waged an internal battle. Part of her didn't want to hear any more. The ugly truth of how blacks were treated in this country was depressing and infuriating. Another part of her wanted to know about Virgil and understood why Demon felt that she *should* know.

She shook her head. "No. I never heard that name."

"Thirteen years old."

That was enough to make Zahra's eyes glaze over.

"After the 16th Street Church bombing," he said, "the one that killed those four little girls, there were a lot of protests and rallies in Birmingham. There were some counter rallies too. Two white boys, both 16 years old, went to a white supremacist rally and bought a confederate flag. They attached it to their scooter and went for a ride – straight to the black part of town. One of 'em had a .22."

The first tear spilled from Zahra's eyes. She did not understand how something that happened so long ago, something she'd never heard of until this moment, was still so dreadfully familiar.

"They saw Virgil and his brother riding a bike," Demon said. "Virgil was sitting on the handlebars. Supposedly, the white boys shot at them to scare 'em, but they ended up killing Virgil. An all-white jury actually convicted them of manslaughter, but they only gave 'em seven months in jail. The judge thought that was too harsh and suspended the sentence, giving them two years of probation instead."

Zahra took a deep breath. She didn't know how to respond to any of this.

"I know you probably think I was wrong when I said I'd be willing to kill a child this morning," Demon said. "To be honest, I was caught up in the moment. I have never harmed anyone who was not my enemy, and I never want to hurt an innocent person. But just like those white people who get radicalized on the internet and end up hating us, I've done enough research to hate them right back. The difference is they got no cause to hate us. They think we're inferior. They think we're violent. They think we're good for nothing, taking away their resources with welfare and Section 8 housing.

"But they can't find nothing on the internet that tells them we been slaughtering them wholesale since the days of slavery, like they been doing us. Despite everything I know, I don't hate all white people. The ones I hate are the ones who hate and want to harm my people for no fucking reason. I do what I do for my uncle and your grandmother and all the other martyrs who never got a hashtag because iPhones didn't exist back then."

With that, he left her alone with her thoughts and the road and her book. When they began speaking again, an hour had passed, and the conversation was lighthearted. Demon asked her to tell him about something embarrassing that happened to her in high school.

Grinning, she asked, "Why you wanna know about something like that?"

"Ain't that what you asked me, a little while back?"
Touché.

She told him about the time a boy named Broderick snatched her ponytail off during lunchtime. Everyone in the cafeteria laughed at her, as he ran around swinging it like a lasso.

Demon said, "If I was there, I woulda kicked his ass."

Zahra was surprised by how good that declaration made her feel.

∞ ∞ ∞ ∞ ∞ ∞ ∞

It was after midnight when they arrived in West Virginia. The group decided to spend the night at a motel in Keystone, which was one of few cities in the state that was predominantly black. On the way to the motel, Zahra was taken aback by the level of poverty, which was apparent despite the darkness concealing most of the eyesores. They spotted a Whataburger and stopped to get enough burgers, fries and drinks for everyone. When they arrived at the motel, they parked near the office and entered together but purchased two rooms. The woman across the counter was curious about that but also grateful to have the money.

"We're traveling together, but I don't like him like that," Zahra offered.

The receptionist laughed at that.

Zahra was bone weary when they climbed the stairs and entered their room. The space was small, with little more than a bed, a dresser and a sofa. Aside from checking to make sure there were no bedbugs – thankfully there were not – Zahra was not concerned with the accommodations. The bed was soft and clean. She couldn't wait to lie down and get some rest. Although Demon had done all of the driving that day, she didn't take a nap during the ride from Georgia. Her grandmother once told her that as a passenger on a road trip, the least she could do was stay up and keep the driver company. That was a lesson that stuck with her.

Tasha and Zulu arrived ten and fifteen minutes later respectively. While they all ate together, Demon teased Zulu about his driving.

"How did I have time to stop for food and get two rooms, and you just now getting here?"

"I had to stop a few times to drain the lizard," Zulu informed him. "Don't know why I insist on drinking energy drinks when I know I'ma be on the road a long time."

"Need to get you some caffeine pills," Demon suggested. "Same effect without the pissing."

Zulu said he'd remember that.

At one a.m. he and Tasha were ready to retire to their rooms. Demon gave Tasha the key to the other room he purchased, while Zulu would sleep in the room he got on the way in.

"What time we heading out?" Tasha asked.

Demon was not apologetic when he replied, "Four am."

"*Damn*," Tasha exclaimed. "Now I'm pissed at Cujo for holding us up this morning, with all his fucking questions."

Zulu laughed at that.

When they were alone, Zahra and Demon showered together. He said it was to save time.

"I might fall asleep if I try to wait for you to get out."

Zahra accepted that, just as she accepted his soft kisses and slippery caresses as the hot water rained down on them. As tired as they both were when they got in the bed, a sweet smile parted her lips when Demon spooned her and asked, "Did you bring another one of them condoms?"

She replied, "If I say yes, are you gon' think I'ma a freak?"

"No. As long as you don't think I'ma a freak for asking if you brought one..."

Zahra did have one. In fact, she had three.

Demon rewarded her for her foresight by licking and sucking her pussy until his face glistened with her essence. He then rolled her to her stomach and entered from behind, while she lie flat on the bed. With her head turned, her eyes half closed, a grateful smile spread across her face, she felt like a lazy lover when he went to work on her wet box. The position didn't require her to move much at all.

Demon didn't seem to mind. He pounded her ass as eagerly as he'd eaten her pussy.

Zahra made a mental note to be the aggressor the next time they made love. And then she came again and couldn't remember what she was supposed to be remembering.

CHAPTER FOURTEEN
MOVING PIECES

The alarm on Demon's cellphone went off at 3:30 am. That gave them thirty minutes to get their things together and head out. Zahra did not feel fatigued when she opened her eyes and sat up in bed. As she took in the unfamiliar surroundings, the reality of what they were doing and why they were there flooded her with adrenaline. Demon disabled the alarm and sent a text message before looking her way. Seeing that she was awake and alert, he said, "How you feeling?" rather than Good morning.

"I'm okay," she said. "I'm good."

He nodded and rolled to the other side of the bed. He sat up and then stood, first stretching his arms over his head and then checking his phone again. Zahra was afforded a few moments to admire his nude physique before he walked to the restroom and disappeared inside.

Thirty minutes later, the team was on the move. Zahra rode shotgun with Tasha this time. Demon and Zulu were both alone in their vehicles. Tasha didn't look sleepy as she exited the motel parking lot, but she was less talkative than usual. Demon called when they made it to the freeway, and Tasha put him on speaker. He opened with the same question he'd asked Zahra that morning.

"Hey, Tasha. How you feeling?"

"I'm tired, but I'll be alright."

"Taking the point position, your role in this might be dangerous," he said. "I need y'all to be careful. Do everything I ask you to do. Remain in communication with me the whole time."

"Did you put the final pieces of your plan together, or do I have to figure out a way to create a *diversion*."

"No. I got it figured out. I'll intercept the Bakers when they leave the trailer park. Me and Zulu will tail them. You and Cleo will stay a few cars ahead. When we get to Clarksburg, we'll go hot when we exit the freeway. You need to get directly in front of them then, even if you have to cut somebody off. When we get to the intersection Sergio's headed to, your car will stall at the red light. Zulu will pull in close behind 'em, boxing them in."

"How's my car gonna stall?"

"You gon' fake it. Just sit there when the light turns green, turn your hazards on if you need to and hold your spot."

"Alright. I can do that."

"While you're waiting, Sergio will be coming in from the west. I'll be parked there too, watching you. Before the light turns red, you need to get the hell outta there. The moment you move, the Bakers will go through the intersection, hoping to catch the light. Or maybe they'll run it, since you held them up so long. Either way, when they pass through the intersection, Sergio will be headed right for them, going full speed. They gon' get T-boned by the 18-wheeler. No way anyone in their truck can survive that."

"Alright," Tasha said again. "Got it."

"Them boys bound to get testy," Demon said. "That's why it might be a little dangerous for y'all. We know they got a short temper, when it come to shit not going their way on the road. They liable to get mad, start blowing they horn and yelling at you. Whatever they do, make sure y'all play it cool. Play dumb. Don't argue with them or antagonize them. The light will only stay green for two minutes. You only need to hold them up for 100 seconds."

"What do we do after we go through the intersection?" Zahra wondered. Tasha hadn't asked, so maybe she already had this intel.

"Go on about your business like you didn't notice an accident behind you," Demon stated. "Make a couple of turns and get back on the freeway. I'll be in touch after I pick up Sergio. We'll head back to Georgia and wait for the news of the Baker brothers' demise. End of story."

He made it sound so simple. Zahra knew it was anything but.

Tasha must have felt the same way because she said, "You know I'll do anything you need me to, but we wouldn't have to go through all this trouble if we'd use a calling card."

"I already floated that idea, several times, and Cujo is against it. I don't remember you having my back then."

"We never put it to a vote."

"Maybe that's something we can talk about after this, but this conversation ain't helping right now."

Tasha shot Zahra a look. Zahra read it well: *This nigga getting testy.*

"Okay," Tasha said with a sigh. "Me and Cleo will be ready for what we gotta do. Good luck with everything on your end."

"Same to you. I'll be in touch," Demon said and then disconnected.

"What's this about a calling card?" Zahra asked. This was the second time she'd heard of it.

"I'll let Demon explain it to you," Tasha said. "It's his idea."

Zahra accepted that and settled in for the ride. This one was much shorter than yesterday. The closer they got to completing this mission, the more anxious she felt.

She told Tasha, "He still hasn't said how Sergio will survive the accident."

"Sometimes you gotta focus on your role and hope everyone else has their roles figured out," Tasha commented.

Zahra mulled that over and decided she could accept that, not that she had any other option.

∞ ∞ ∞ ∞ ∞ ∞ ∞

The drive from Keystone to Gilmer County was three hours, which explained why Demon wanted to roll out so early. They'd arrive in the vicinity of the Baker brother's trailer park at seven a.m. From there, the courthouse in Clarksville was an hour away. Based on their cellphone data from the previous weeks, Demon knew the brothers usually left their home and headed to court at 7:15. His timing would give his crew a fifteen-minute head start.

Communication between the group was minimal as they traveled to the trailer park. Tasha was usually energetic and talkative, but she only responded to the few questions Zahra asked during the drive, rather than spark a conversation of her own. Zahra couldn't tell if she was in the zone or fatigued from the night of little rest. Either way, she quieted down after a while and left Tasha to her thoughts.

When they arrived in Gilmer County, Demon called again.

"How y'all holding up?"

"Man, I'm just driving," Tasha reported. "Think I'm on autopilot. But we made it."

Demon instructed them to remain on the interstate for ten more miles and then take the third exit. "There's a RaceTrac off Grandcamp Run. I want y'all to wait there until you hear from me. Zulu's stopping too. But he'll be at a different gas station."

"Got it. Is it okay if we get out, to get some coffee or something?"

"Yeah, that's cool. Your part in this still works if you get caught on camera, same for Zulu."

"I know he glad to hear that," Tasha joked. "That nigga prolly dying to take a piss."

Zahra laughed at that.

The first sign of trouble came when Demon called again fifteen minutes later. He told them, "Hold on a sec, let me get Zulu on the line with us." After a few moments, he said, "Alright, is everyone here?" Both the ladies and Zulu confirmed they were on the line.

"It's time to get moving," Demon said, "but before you do, I need to tell you the Baker brothers aren't alone. I pulled into the trailer park, put on a utility worker vest and a hardhat and pretended to be checking the meters while I waited for 'em. They got in their truck with another man, older, and a woman who looked about their age. I'm guessing that's one of their wives or girlfriends. As far as the dude, I don't know who he is. Their father is in prison. Could be an uncle, or just some random. If we do this, *all of 'em gon' die.* I need to know if y'all cool with that, or if you wanna abort. Normally I'd be okay with a majority opinion, but for this, it needs to be unanimous."

Zahra looked Tasha's way, and Tasha looked at her. They were both present when Demon said he was willing to kill one of the brothers' children. According to Demon, they would probably grow to be racist just like their dad. But Tasha wasn't around when Demon somewhat retracted his statement. He told Zahra he'd never killed an innocent person and did not plan to do so.

"Without a blind vote," Demon continued, "I know you could be influenced by whoever votes first. But I need all of you to vote with your heart. Vote your *conscious.* Cleo, since you new, I think you should go first."

Zulu cast his vote, as if he hadn't heard him. "Fuck it. I'm down. If they rolling with them Bakers, that means they down with 'em. Fuck everybody who support them crackers. Let's do it."

Zahra realized Demon was right about the influence the first vote would have over the others. She was *almost* sure she would've made the same decision without hearing from Zulu first, but almost wasn't 100%.

"I'm down," she said, her apprehension wreaking havoc on her pulse.

"You sure?" Demon asked.

"Yeah. I'm sure."

"I'm down too," Tasha said. "I didn't do all this fucking driving for nothing."

"It ain't about the driving," Demon said.

"I know. I'm just kidding. I know this ain't no time for jokes, but that's how I deal with my stress sometimes. Even if we only drove a block, I'd still say let's do it. Zulu's right. Any supporter of them is an enemy of mine. I'm ready."

"Alright," Demon said. "Then y'all need to get moving, *pronto*. They on the move. I'm on their tail. It's an hour drive, so you got plenty time to catch up with them, but I'd feel better if y'all was closer."

"I'm leaving the gas station now," Tasha reported, "'bout to get back on 79."

"Perfect, I'll call you back in a little bit," Demon said. "Y'all some down ass soldiers. I knew I picked the right crew for this."

He ended the call.

∞ ∞ ∞ ∞ ∞ ∞ ∞

It took a bit of coordination with both drivers before Demon got everyone into position. Tasha was masterful behind the wheel. Zahra watched with admiration as she caught up with Demon on the interstate, and they laid eyes on the Baker brother's truck for the first time. It was nothing fancy, a dusty quad-cab F-150 with most of its better days behind it. Zahra's blood raced when they pulled alongside the truck before taking the lead in a small convoy the Bakers didn't realize they were now part of. It took a lot of willpower for Zahra to ignore the people in the truck when they passed it. Tasha was more seasoned. She stared straight ahead. She even bobbed her head to nonexistent music. She appeared perfectly casual.

Nothing to see here, folks. Just a couple of black chicks out for a morning drive – not plotting your doom at all.

Rather than move in front of the truck, Tasha remained in the lane next to them and continued to speed up, until she was several car lengths ahead. Traffic was light. Zahra wasn't sure if that was a good thing, but when Demon called again, he approved of everything they had done thus far.

"Tasha, you're doing good. Hold your position. It doesn't look like they're in too big of a hurry. We got a while to go before we get off the freeway. If they speed up, go ahead and let them pass you. We can make it up later on down the road. Zulu, you can hang back a little more, but keep your eyes on 'em. I'll let you know when it's time to get on their ass."

"Bet," Zulu replied.

"Cleo, you still up?" Demon asked.

"You know I'm up. I couldn't sleep right now if I wanted to."

"This'll be over soon. I'ma call Sergio, see how things are going on his end. I'll holler at y'all in a little bit."

When he disconnected, Tasha mocked him. "*Cleo, you still up?* Nigga didn't ask if *I* was up."

Zahra chuckled nervously. "I think he know you still up, seeing as how we haven't slid off the side of the road."

"Mmmm hmmm," Tasha hummed snarkily, but she was grinning. "Who would've ever thought Demon would find love – with somebody in our group?"

177

Despite the intimate moments they'd shared, Zahra couldn't say that Demon *had* found love. But she didn't deny the possibility. Instead, she asked, "You surprised that he likes me?"

"No, not that he likes *you*. I'm surprised that he likes *anybody*. Demon one of those dudes that's so focused on the culture and his missions that he don't seem to have eyes for anything else. All I've ever seen him passionate about is his books and those message boards he's always reading. He's proof positive that you don't have to go to college to be a scholar. He'll tell you some shit off the top of his head that'll make you swear this nigga's a walking encyclopedia."

Zahra smiled at that. "I was thinking the same thing, not too long ago."

"But it's good though, whatever's going on between you and him. Everybody need somebody."

Zahra started to tell her that she and Demon were not a couple, but she knew Tasha would roll her eyes at that. They'd spent the night together in a small hotel room with only one bed. She remained silent and let the conversation die.

∞ ∞ ∞ ∞ ∞ ∞ ∞

Everything was going smoothly an hour later when Demon called back with another issue that wasn't necessarily cause for alarm, but he thought they should keep it on the radar. By then they were five minutes away from Clarksburg.

"Y'all noticing a lot of bumper stickers?" he asked, again on speaker. His voice had hints of concern as it wafted from the car's stereo system.

178

Tasha looked over at Zahra curiously. Zahra shook her head.

Zulu said, "Yeah, I seen some. Lotta Trump supporters in these parts."

Zahra began to look around. She only saw one car with a bumper sticker in support of the disgraced former president.

"Could be nothing," Demon said. "But all the ones I seen are headed the same direction as us. Some of 'em could be headed to the courthouse."

"West Virginia been a red state for the past twenty years," Zulu said. "In 2020, 70% of 'em voted republican."

"I'm hoping that's all it is," Demon said.

"Why does it worry you?" Zahra asked.

"'Cause if some of 'em headed to the courthouse to show support for the Bakers, they might cause a problem for us. I don't know how, but I don't put nothing past these rednecks. I guess I'm more worried about you and Tasha. When y'all pull your little trick at that intersection, ain't no telling what these folks will do."

"Cars break down every day," Tasha said. "They can't get mad at us. What's the worst that can happen?"

"You know I hate when you say that."

"I know," she said. "I'm sorry."

Demon sighed and then said, "Fuck it. We almost there. Tasha, go ahead and make your move. We got two more exits before we get off the freeway. You need to be right in front of 'em when we do."

"Alright. I'm moving now."

"I'm closing in, too" Zulu said

"The freeway makes a loop when you get off," Demon informed them, "then you'll be going south on Chestnut. We gon' hit 'em at *Chestnut and Pike.* That'll be the first light you get to. Tasha, don't let nobody get in between y'all."

"Don't worry," she told him. "This gon' go down exactly like you planned it."

But she was wrong about that.

Tasha successfully got into position before they exited the freeway. Zulu merged and got behind the brothers. The three vehicles made the loop Demon told them about and continued on Chestnut. Zahra watched the truck through the side mirror but couldn't get a good look at everyone inside. Tasha could see them a lot better in the rearview mirror.

"It's four of 'em in the truck," she reported, "just like Demon said. One of the brothers is driving, with the old man sitting up front."

Zahra didn't respond, other than nodding.

Tasha told her, "Breathe, girl."

Zahra's eyes remained fixed on the side mirror. "I am breathing."

"Breathe slower. Slow inhale, slow exhale."

Zahra took her advice, and she felt a little better.

As they approached Pike, Zahra saw that the light was green. Tasha had plenty of time to make it, but she slowed down. Zahra watched the light with unblinking eyes as it turned yellow. Behind them, someone honked their horn.

"Damn. I thought they'd wait for us to stall in the middle of the street before they got uptight," Tasha said, mostly to herself. "This still works though..."

She slowed down and came to a stop, rather than try to make the light. The Baker's truck was right on her ass. Zulu was on theirs.

"Perfect," Tasha said.

They waited.

The intersection had two lane streets in both directions, so there was no one on their right or left. Ahead of them, there was one car facing them, also parked at the light. There was a light flow of traffic moving east and west. Zahra thought they had somehow missed their mark when she saw a semi-truck pass through the intersection, but it wasn't barreling down the road at breakneck speeds, and it was traveling west. She knew Sergio would be coming from the opposite direction.

They waited.

The 120 seconds the light was supposed to remain red felt like an eternity, but eventually it turned green. Tasha got moving again, and then she abruptly slammed the brakes, midway through the intersection. The horn behind her immediately blared again as the driver narrowly avoided rear-ending her. First there were a couple of honks, and then the driver held the horn for five good seconds.

Tasha remained focused and seemingly calm. She reached and pressed a button on the dash to activate her hazard lights. The driver behind them tried to back up, but Zulu had them boxed in. The driver of the truck laid on the horn again to no avail. Zahra looked back and locked eyes with the man. She could tell by his gesticulations that he was becoming irate. She wondered if this was how quickly he got upset with Jaylen Campbell on that dark, county road almost one year ago. She looked at Tasha. She was staring at her rearview mirror. Zahra's breaths were hot and audible. She checked the intersection again and spotted Demon. He pulled up from the east side and stopped at the light. From that distance, Zahra couldn't make out his features, but she knew he was watching them.

Behind them, the driver's side door of the pickup truck flew open. Tasha killed the engine as the driver approached on her side. When he came into view, Zahra saw that he was dressed in a suit. It didn't fit well, and he had no tie. He was clean-shaven, and his hair was combed, but he still reeked of white trash. The suit did little to hide his tan skin, which had a leathery texture. She saw a tattoo on his neck that was mostly concealed by the collar of his shirt. Even with the window up, she and Tasha heard him clearly when he spoke to them.

"The hell is going on?"

Aside from the fact that he was being set up for a gruesome murder, Zahra wondered how he could be so upset at eight o'clock in the morning. He was on his way to court for a road rage incident that ended in murder. Had the ordeal taught him nothing?

Tasha moved to roll her window down, but with no power, the button was useless. She yelled back at him through the window.

"My car went dead!"

"How the hell your car went dead? And why'd you stop the first time? You could've made the light."

Behind them another door opened, this time on the truck's passenger side. Zahra looked back and saw the older man exit the vehicle. He wore a full beard and wasn't dressed as nice. He reminded her of one of the country bumpkins from Duck Dynasty.

"I don't know what's wrong with it!" Tasha yelled at the one standing beside her door. She appeared every bit as flustered as you would expect under these circumstances.

"Open your door!" the man yelled back at her.

"What I'ma open my door for? I don't know you!"

"Open your door and let me try to help get your car started!"

"I ain't opening my door!"

"Well, pop the hood!"

The one talking to Tasha was getting red about the face. The other one was closing in on Zahra's side of the car. She heard him ask the driver, "What's going on?"

"Dumbass says her car won't start."

"Can y'all get away from my car?" Tasha shouted. "You freaking me out!"

"Get your car out the road!" the younger one yelled. "I got somewhere to be!"

"Hold on, let me..."

Tasha pressed her foot on the brake and then pushed the button to start the car. It started right up.

"*For fucking sake!*" the one in the suit said, throwing his hands up.

Tasha put her car in gear and threw a parting shot at him. "Fuck you!"

As they drove away, Zahra turned completely around in her seat and watched the men return to their truck. A moment later, they began to roll through the intersection. So caught up with the unexpected drama, Zahra had almost forgotten that something major was supposed to happen until it did. The Ford was exactly midway through the intersection when something big, fast and mean suddenly appeared from the west, traveling at well over sixty miles per hour. Her eyes and mouth flashed open at the same time when the 18-wheeler slammed into the smaller truck with enough force to immediately send it flying from her field of view.

183

The collision was so sudden, so brutal, and so explosive, Zahra half expected an actual explosion, but it was nothing like that. One second the truck was behind them. She could still see that the driver was still irritated. The next second, the truck had been wiped out. There was a loud CRACK of metal impacting unyielding metal, and then both vehicles were gone. In their place, she could see Zulu's car again. He hadn't moved an inch.

"*Shit*," Zahra breathed.

"*Oh, my God, that was crazy,*" Tasha uttered, her eyes glued to the rearview mirror. She shook her head in wonderment. "Demon was right. Ain't no way nobody–"

PAT-PAT! PAT! PAT! PAT!

"*The fuck was that?*" Tasha exclaimed.

Even though the sound was distant, Zahra was pretty sure she knew exactly what it was. She suspected Tasha did too.

"Somebody shooting," she said, her eyes growing frantic.

"Who shooting?" Tasha wondered. "Ain't nobody supposed to be shooting..."

By then they had reached Main Street, and Tasha was forced to turn left or right. Before she made the turn, Zahra heard tires squealing. A second later, Demon's car burst through the intersection, traveling west, the direction Sergio's truck had come. All the muscle his Charger could provide was on display as he zoomed past.

PAT! PAT!

"*Who's shooting?*" Tasha asked again.

"*I don't know! I don't see nobody!*"

184

"*Fuck...*" Tasha sat at the T-intersection and turned in her seat. From that distance, they could still make out Zulu's car but little else.

"Ain't nobody supposed to be shooting," she said again. She locked eyes with Zahra. "Demon said something to you about shooting?"

"No. He didn't say anything."

Tasha shook her head. Zahra had never seen her frazzled, but Tasha couldn't hide her unease as she checked the road ahead of them before reluctantly making a right turn.

CHAPTER FIFTEEN
THE FINAL CHAPTER
CALLING CARD

Despite the dramatic scene Tasha and Zahra had witnessed, Demon was calm when he called them five minutes later.

"Hey, I need y'all to scoop me up. My shit's hot. Gotta ditch this ride."

Zahra was flooded with relief when she heard his voice on speaker.

"What happened?" Tasha asked, her voice filled with concern. "We heard shooting. And we saw you peel off. You okay?"

"I'm fine," Demon said. "But I told y'all I had a bad feeling about all those damn bumper stickers. Some Good Samaritan pulled over and started chasing Sergio when he bailed out the truck. When he couldn't catch up to him, he started shooting. Shit was wild."

Zahra shook her head in disbelief. *Shit was wild* was a huge understatement.

"*A Good Samaritan?*" Tasha repeated.

186

"I should've ran his dumb ass over," Demon said. "Letting off shots at my nigga like that. Ran me hot. I drove right past him and went to get my boy."

"Is Sergio alright?" Zahra asked.

"Yeah. He didn't get hit. Got some road rash from bailing out of that semi, but he's alright. I told you this boy's a trooper."

"How did he—"

Demon cut Tasha off. "We gon' have to finish this conversation when I see you. Right now I'm headed to a parking garage downtown. I know some people saw me pick up Sergio. Plus I got caught on that red light camera. I'ma send you the address to this garage. You need to get here *pronto*. Ain't nobody following us, but police gon' be looking for this car."

"Alright," Tasha said. "Send me the address."

"Sending it now."

When he hung up, Tasha looked over at her passenger. Even though Zahra was relieved, she still looked spooked.

"Yo man be getting involved in some crazy shit," Tasha said, shaking her head. "Sergio bailed out of the truck... I don't know why, but I thought he was still in it."

"Have you ever met Sergio?"

"No. But I'm dying to meet him now. I bet he look like a Mexican Rambo."

She got a notification on her phone. She checked it and saw the address Demon wanted them to head to. It was only a few minutes away from their current location. She called Zulu as she headed that way.

"Hey," he answered.

"You heard from Demon?"

187

"Yeah. Just got off the phone with him. He told you what happened?"

"Mmm hmm. I'm still trying to wrap my mind around it. Me and Cleo on our way to pick them up. You okay?"

"I'm fine," Zulu said. "Just watched one of the craziest things I've ever seen. Ya boy Demon is a straight up *menace*. Sergio, he a real one."

"Where you headed now?"

"Columbus."

"*Columbus*?"

"Demon said he had a change of plans, as far as getting back to Georgia. We flying now."

Zahra was surprised and grateful to hear that. After all they'd experienced, she was not looking forward to the long drive back to Atlanta.

"What about our rides?" Tasha asked.

"He said we're gonna leave 'em at the airport for now. Come back later and set up another tactical point up north."

"Good," Tasha said. "We *been* needing to do that. I'm almost at this parking garage. We'll call you back once we get Demon."

"A'ight. Holler."

∞ ∞ ∞ ∞ ∞ ∞ ∞

They found Demon and Sergio on the third level. Demon exited the Charger wearing latex gloves, so Zahra knew that he'd wiped it down. He went to the trunk and grabbed his duffle bag before heading their way. The man he was with also wore a pair of gloves. Sergio looked nothing like Zahra or Tasha expected. He was short, remarkably so,

188

and clean shaven, other than a thin moustache. He was dark-skinned and a little pudgy. As he climbed into the backseat, Zahra noticed his jeans were soiled, and he had road rash on both arms. But all things considered, he looked fairly well.

"Preciate the ride," Demon said as he slid in behind Tasha. "I'm ready to get the hell outta this state."

Zahra's smile was endearing as she looked back at him. "I'm glad y'all made it. You had us worried."

"I ain't gon' lie, I was a little worried too," Demon said as Tasha got moving. He sighed and looked over at Sergio. "This the man who deserves all the credit. Sergio, this is Tasha and Cleo."

"Nice to meet y'all," the man said. His accent was southern with barely any trace of his Hispanic heritage.

"Please tell me how you managed to jump out of that truck without breaking your neck," Tasha said. "I saw how fast it was going."

He told them, "It wasn't going that fast when I jumped out. I found a toolbox in the cab. It was little but heavy. I put it on the gas pedal right before I jumped, figured the accident would be so bad, the toolbox would probably get tossed around. They would think it fell from somewhere in the back."

"That's smart thinking, ain't it?" Demon said. "I didn't come up with that."

Zahra nodded as she watched them.

"I got a little scratched up," Sergio said, examining his arms. "Could've been worse. The trick is to hit the ground rolling and keep your head tucked."

Zahra's bewilderment continued to grow. "Sounds like you've done that before."

189

"I've done some jobs as a wheelman," Sergio acknowledged. "Did some time for it too. Guess we all got a past, right?"

Zahra didn't have a response for that. The more Sergio talked, the more she realized he was far more complex than his appearance projected.

"What about the truck?" Tasha asked. "They can't trace that back to you?"

Demon said, "Now you know me better than that. When have I ever put someone in a vehicle that could get traced back to us?"

"I'm just saying. That's a big ass truck..."

"That's something you don't have to worry about," he assured her.

"The guy that was shooting," Tasha said, "you said it was just some random?"

"This is *West Virginia*," Demon reminded her. "You know these white folks out here looking for a reason to shoot a black or brown person."

"My thinking was," Sergio said, "if somebody saw me jump out, I would tell them my brakes failed, and I knew there was gonna be an accident. But this asshole got out of his car with a gun in his hand. I barely made it to my feet, and he's ready to do a citizen's arrest, or whatever he was thinking. To be honest, I didn't think he'd start shooting when I took off, but sure enough, he tried to take me out." He smacked his lips. "It's all good, though. Ain't the first time."

Zahra could do nothing but shake her head and blink at him. She felt like if they talked to Sergio for an hour, he'd entertain them with a litany of bizarre things he'd done that weren't his *first time*.

"I got some people in my group who don't trust you 'cause you not an official member," Demon told his friend. "I ain't saying it's either of these ladies, but for the record, could you tell them why you're always down when I call you?"

Sergio's tone had been lighthearted until Demon posed that question. Zahra watched his features darken. He was somber when he responded.

"August 3rd, 2019. Asshole walked into a Walmart in El Paso with the intent to kill as many Mexicans as possible. Body count was twenty-three, with just as many injured. He came all the way from Allen, Texas to do that. Said immigrants was trying to replace white people and take their resources. The thing about white nationalists is they don't just hate black people. They may have done more shit to y'all over the years, but they hate us just as much. And they hate the Jews, which I don't understand, 'cause every Jew I ever met looks like a white man to me. I'm down with y'all because we all in the same boat. We got the same enemy."

Demon nodded his approval.

Zahra knew about the shooting he was referring to. The familiarity of the El Paso shooting made her think of her grandmother. Sergio locked eyes with her and noticed hers had filled with tears. He thought they were for the Hispanic victims he'd mentioned. She didn't correct him.

They drove in silence for a while before Tasha tried to lighten the mood and the direction of the conversation.

"Zulu said we headed to Columbus, what's up with that?"

"Yeah, Columbus International," Demon said. "We gon' leave our cars at the airport. I'll bring a team out in a few days to move them to a storage unit. We need to set up something around here. Them eight, nine-hour drives is played out."

"You ain't never lying," Tasha quipped.

"We'll fly back to Georgia, take an Uber to pick up the rentals, and then fly back to Houston. We'll get back pretty late, but at least we won't be on the road the whole time."

"That'll work," Tasha said. She pulled up the airport on her phone and saw that it was a three-hour drive.

"We need to stop at a Walmart when we get to Ohio," Demon said. "Get Sergio some new clothes and some Band-Aids, some Neosporin or something."

"*Band-Aids*?" Tasha exclaimed. "Look like he need some *bandages* – and some *gauze*."

Demon smacked his lips. "Whatever. You know what I meant."

"I bet you one of them old-school niggas that think Robitussin can fix *anything*."

"It can," he said. "I sprained my ankle when I was in middle school. Mama gave me some Robitussin; I was as good as new."

Zahra laughed, hoping he was joking about that. But he said it with such a straight face, she couldn't be sure.

∞ ∞ ∞ ∞ ∞ ∞ ∞

The ride to Columbus was short by comparison but still long. With Demon and Sergio in the car, Zahra didn't think she was solely responsible for keeping the driver company, so she got a good nap. Thanks to Head, their plane tickets were waiting on them when they arrived at the airport. Demon, Zulu, Tasha, and Zahra flew back to Atlanta. Sergio's plane was headed to El Paso. This made

Zahra wonder if he'd lost someone in the mass murder he told them about, but she didn't ask.

It was close to ten p.m. when they made it back to Houston. By then the news from West Virginia was making the cycle on most major networks. The accident alone was enough to garnish the attention of reporters who were eager to give America its latest dose of Final Destination-style macabre. Once the identity of the victims was revealed, the story grew legs, adding another layer to the attention-grabbing headlines.

Some speculated that this may be a case of retribution, especially when you consider the truck driver who leapt from the vehicle as it torpedoed towards the Baker brothers and then fled on foot. Who was this man? Why did he run, and where did he go? The semi-truck was not reported stolen until after the accident. Was this because the owner did not realize it was missing, or were they somehow involved? The driver who disappeared from the scene was described as Hispanic, which fit the image of a truck driver but not the expectation of someone who had a grievance with the Baker brothers.

Taken at face value, a truck driver lost control of his vehicle, knew an accident was imminent, and cowardly decided to save his own ass and avoid prosecution. But the internet was full of conspiracy theorists who had decided that was exactly what the truck driver wanted you to think. The police vowed to continue their investigation and determine if the accident that took the lives of four individuals was truly an accident. Zahra knew the public shouldn't hold their breath while waiting for their findings.

With so much news coverage, she wasn't surprised to see Demon engaged in mildly heated conversations on the phone during their trip home. It seemed as if the only time he wasn't explaining himself to the caller was when they were on an airplane and there was no cellular service. Zahra did not have to ask who he was speaking to. As far as she knew, Cujo was the only person who held Demon's feet to the fire like this.

She and Demon returned to the H-town headquarters alone. Zulu and Tasha went their separate ways when they left the airport. Zahra expected Cujo to be there. He'd want to continue the discussion in person. But the house was empty. Even the computer guys had called it quits a few hours ago. Zahra considered this a blessing. She was too tired to be cordial. Too sleepy to entertain anyone. She showered and felt like she was in a trance when she made her way to the bed.

Before drifting off, Demon told her, "We're having a meeting tomorrow. Everyone will be here. You finally get to meet the whole group."

She simply responded, "Okay."

He got in bed with her, and, for the first time since she'd known him, he did not check his phone before following her to dream land. They'd both had enough drama for the day.

∞ ∞ ∞ ∞ ∞ ∞ ∞

They slept, uninterrupted, for ten full hours. When they awakened, the sun was bright and beautiful. Zahra felt content and refreshed. She made breakfast, and they ate together. Satisfied with each other's company and the alone time they were afforded, they didn't talk much during the meal. The meeting Demon told her about was scheduled for six o'clock. Until then, they didn't have any pressing matters to attend to. Demon spent a lot of time in the computer room researching the next list of targets. Zahra lounged on the futon in the same room, happy to get back to Fred Hampton and the Civil War book he had given her.

At four o'clock, members of the group began to show up. By six p.m., they were all there, minus Sergio, who wasn't an official member for some reason. With everyone gathered in the living room, Zahra took her time studying them. Like Head and Einstein, it seemed as if they all came from different walks of life. Most were young, under the age of 40, and most of them were men. Zahra had greeted them as they arrived at the headquarters. They all knew of her and offered condolences for her grandmother. They said they were glad to have her aboard. She replied that she was happy to be there.

She knew the meeting was called to discuss the differences of opinion Cujo and Demon had been having. It was no surprise to see the two of them standing before the group, while everyone else was seated, some on the couch, some on barstools, others had brought chairs in from the dining room.

"Thank you all for showing up today," Cujo said, starting the meeting. "It's good to see all of us in one place at the same time. We should do this more often, but I understand why it's not feasible most of the time."

Everyone watched him, some nodded their agreement.

"The reason I called you in today," Cujo continued, "is to discuss what happened yesterday and ask you to participate in a formal vote, to determine the direction we'll go in the future. You know about the mission Demon pulled off in West Virginia. By now, I'm sure you've seen the reports on the news. Personally, I don't like it when anything we do makes the news. Our group is founded on *secrecy*. No one is supposed to know we exist. I think that what happened yesterday, while it didn't put any of our names in the paper, brought more attention to what we're doing than anything has before." He looked to Demon. "You got anything you wanna add?"

Demon shook his head. He didn't look upset about the direction the meeting was going.

"For the sake of transparency," Cujo went on, "I told Demon I didn't think this latest mission was a good idea. I told him this in the days leading up to it and the day before. In the end, I gave him my blessing, mostly because I saw that he wasn't backing down – but that's beside the point. What's important is I supported the mission, so I take full responsibility for how it played out. I don't want y'all to think I'm coming down on Demon, or there's a rift in the group."

Zahra thought he was double-talking them now. The first time she met Cujo, she sensed he would be a hard person to like. She'd tried to move past their initial awkward introduction, but he wasn't making it easy for her.

Demon spoke up. "Can I say something?"

Cujo quickly nodded. "Yeah, man. Of course."

Demon looked over the room slowly. He briefly locked eyes with Zahra. She saw that he was doing the same with all of the others.

"What happened yesterday," he said, "is a direct result of a philosophy we've been abiding by, something I've been against for quite a while. Like Cujo said, our group is founded on secrecy. That's not something I want to change.

196

I don't want anyone to know any of our names. But I don't think the methods we use to accomplish our missions have to be shrouded in secrecy. There's a difference between no one knowing who we are versus no one knowing what we do.

"We've taken out a lot of targets. I'm happy with the success we've had, but when you look at the time we've invested to come up with these *elaborate plots*, hell, we prolly could've taken out twice as many. Yesterday we had to knock off two people, in the middle of the street, in broad daylight. Watching the news, it may seem like we lost control, and things got out of hand. But that job went down exactly like I planned it. Not one thing happened yesterday that I hadn't accounted for."

"So, you think it was a success?" Cujo interjected.

"Yes, it was a success," Demon said. "As much of a success as it could've been under those circumstances. But the thing is *we are the ones creating the circumstances*, so why are we making this so hard on ourselves? I was at their trailer park that morning. I could've put a bullet in both their heads and dipped. I could've did that *alone*. The four people I had with me could've been somewhere else taking out four more targets."

"Okay, now we're getting to the meat of the disagreement we're having," Cujo said. "Demon is ready to basically go live with this, start leaving bodies that will be connected sooner or later, and the feds will be looking for us."

"I don't need you to tell them what I'm ready to do," Demon said, frowning.

Cujo took a step back, nodding. "Okay. Okay."

"I been telling y'all we should leave a calling card," Demon said.

Cujo stepped forward again, mouth open. Demon gave him a look, and Cujo closed his mouth, nodding again.

"Alright, so here's the deal," Demon said, addressing the group. "These people we're after, they're not getting the picture. I go on their message boards every day. Every day there's more of 'em. Some of 'em just talking shit. Internet gangstas. But some of 'em are the real deal. They're getting radicalized. I'm watching it happen – in real time. Won't be long before they go out and get an AR and do something stupid.

"We're doing a good job. But why aren't we trying to send a message? We should be letting them know that we're coming for 'em and taking 'em out. Think about it: What if I would've killed them boys at the trailer park and left a card, then went on the internet and let the world know what that card means? What if we do that ten more times, fifty more times, leave the same card every time. Now they got something to fear. Now they gotta think twice before they get back on those hate sites talking reckless."

Cujo could hold his peace no longer. "And the feds will be on our ass quicker than you can turn around. Once you give the police a target, something they can zero in on, how long do you think it'll take for them to find us? Name one serial killer who left *notes* and got away with it. The feds used those notes to find them *every single time*."

"Those killers were dumb," Demon countered. "They were sending notes to the press, playing with the police, antagonizing them. Ain't nobody in this room that stupid. I'm not talking about a note you have to print or mail or nothing like that. I'm talking something simple, like the mafia used to do when they left a fish on your porch. Everybody who got that fish knew what was up. And you wanna go after a *whole militia*, so I don't know why you don't see that what I'm saying makes sense. *We can't kill twenty people secretly.* But we can kill twenty people and leave a calling card. Fuck it if the world knows they're connected. I want 'em to know. Just like when the Klan was burning crosses in people's yards. They *wanted* them to know they were a target. We need to stop hiding and make a statement."

"This is what you're all here for," Cujo said. "Demon and I want to go in opposite directions, so we have to have a vote. I say we leave things the way they are. No attention, no connections between these killings. Ain't no police looking for us *yet*. Demon's plan will change that. I think the police *and* the people we're after will be looking for us."

"And I say we go live" Demon said. "These crackers need to know that if they keep up that bullshit, we coming for 'em. Ain't that what they used to do to us? You keep trying to vote, we coming for you. You trying to integrate, we coming for you. They need a taste of their own medicine. We can't make people change their behavior by doing this anonymously."

"How we gon' handle this?" Cujo asked him.

"Blind," Demon said. "Everybody pull out your phone. Send me a text message. Either say 'Keep it the same,' or 'Calling card.' Those are the only options. Me and Cujo gon' leave the room, but don't talk to each other about this. Don't ask nobody what they're voting."

"Are we going with the majority?" Cujo asked him.

Demon shook his head. "No. Not for my plan. In order for calling card to win, we need a *two-thirds* majority. You're right about this move increasing our risk, so it can't be just half of us who's down with that."

Cujo nodded and led the way out of the room. "We'll be back to tell you how the vote went once we get them all in."

Everyone watched them go and then looked around at each other. No one said a word as they looked down at their phones. Some began typing immediately. Others considered their options and took a while longer to make a decision.

EPILOGUE

Neither Demon nor Cujo appeared upset when they returned to the group five minutes later to deliver the results of the vote. Afterwards, in a show of solidarity, they worked side-by-side in the kitchen, making dinner for everyone. No one was allowed to assist in the preparation of the meal. They wouldn't even let Tasha chop veggies for the salad.

Dinner that night was fried catfish with seasoned fries. It was delicious. Everyone thought their two default leaders did an amazing job. Zahra had been in the kitchen a few times, but there was one cabinet she'd never opened. She thought it housed pots and pans, but it was actually filled with various bottles of alcohol. With the liquor flowing and music playing, a party atmosphere ensued and lasted late into the night. Only a few people left afterwards. The rest found a place to sleep, either in one of the bedrooms or the pull-out sofas.

When Zahra and Demon retreated to their room after midnight, they were both a little tipsy but not drunk. Emboldened by the tequila in her system, she waited in bed naked while he showered. He emerged from the bathroom wearing only his boxers. Upon seeing her, his eyes darkened, and his manhood began to rise.

She sat up and scooted to the edge of the bed, her eyes sultry, and her legs spread. She told him, "David, I'm starting to think you don't want me to suck your dick."

His eyes narrowed. A slight grin curved the corner of his mouth. "What gives you that idea?"

"I guess 'cause you've never put your dick in my mouth." Her smile was mischievous.

"I didn't want to be too bold," he replied. "Or presumptuous. I didn't know if it was okay to do that."

"What kind of invitation you need?"

She slid off the bed, down to her knees. She was now eye-to-eye with his boxers. His piece continued to swell, stretching the fabric. He watched her and then looked towards the door. The sound of conversations and laughter was still prevalent, both upstairs and downstairs.

He asked her, "Is the door locked?"

She nodded and reached for his boxers. She pulled them all the way down his legs and assisted as he stepped out of them. Now that they were both nude, she looked up at him and smiled. He was rock hard now. She caressed him with both hands, enjoying the heat radiating from his piece and the pleasure she was giving him. Demon's eyes were half-closed, glazed, lost in lust. His hand moved to her shoulder and then tentatively to the side of her face. Slowly his fingers made their way to the back of her head and urged her forward. She opened her mouth and tongue kissed the tip of his dick. Demon wanted to keep quiet, but he couldn't stop a surprised and grateful grunt from escaping him.

Encouraged by his desire, she took him in deeper, all the way to the back of her throat. He pulled out and allowed her to concentrate her soft lips and hot tongue on the head before he slid in again, all the way to her tonsils. She looked up at him when he caught a steady rhythm and began to pump slowly. She saw that he was watching her. For him, the look in her eyes and the sight of his dick disappearing inside her mouth was enough to stimulate electric synapses of pleasure that had him ready to explode, even though only one minute had passed.

She tasted his pre cum. Her eyes slipped closed as she swallowed it and sucked harder. She backed away and looked up at him again, her warm breath bathing his piece as it pulsated in her face.

"David, are you gonna cum in my mouth?"

He didn't know how to respond to that. This was too much. This whole day was, but this... His breath came in shudders. She took him into her mouth again, stroking him with her hand and her jaws.

Demon was never able to articulate a response to her question, but actions speak louder than words. He held her head with both hands when his climax reached a crescendo. She kept sucking and swallowing. Sucking and swallowing. Her jaws were not tired when he was spent, so she kept sucking, hoping he'd give her more to swallow.

When she finally released him and looked up again, she saw that his mouth hung open. Every muscle in his body was relaxed – except his dick. It remained rock hard.

She returned to the bed, crawling on her hands and knees, with her back to him. She spread her legs and lowered her head, until only her ass was poking up. Demon stood there, staring at his offering for so long, she wondered if he had anything left in the tank.

But then he said, "Please tell me you got another one of those condoms." His voice was breathy, barely above a whisper.

Grinning, she replied with the same hushed tone. "In the dresser. Top drawer on the right..."

∞ ∞ ∞ ∞ ∞ ∞ ∞

One week later, in the beautiful city of Long Beach, California, William Burke set the alarm for his small bar on Euclid Avenue before stepping outside the front entrance and locking the doors. At 2:30 a.m. on a balmy Tuesday night, the streets were empty, the area calm and peaceful. William was not wary as he checked to make sure the door was secure before walking down the sidewalk and making a left around the building, towards the parking lot.

His bar didn't bring in a shitload of money that night, but it was a respectable day's work. In any event, he'd left the day's earnings in a safe that few knew he had in his office. The safe was bolted to the building, so there was no chance of a thief making off with it, if someone decided to break into the bar in the wee hours of the morning. The safe was also fireproof, so he did not fear losing the money due to a natural or manmade disaster. In the morning, he would return to work, retrieve the money, and take it to the bank when the sun was out, and the streets were populated, and the chance of getting robbed had decreased tenfold.

Despite these precautions, *robbery* was the first thing on his mind when he heard quick footsteps approaching him as he walked to his Jeep Wrangler, which was the only car in the parking lot. His heart froze, but his body did not. He moved his keys to his left hand and reached for his concealed pistol with his right. He almost had time to draw the weapon when a voice behind him, which was now much closer, said, "Don't try it. I already got mine pointed at your head. You not gon' have time to turn around, before I pull the trigger."

Judging by the sound and dialect of the voice, William knew that the man who had accosted him was black. That was not a surprising or even disappointing observation. It would've been surprising if this was not the case.

William heard more footsteps.

The person behind him said, "Take your hand away from your gun and hold both hands down to your sides."

William obeyed these instructions. He said, "I don't have any money on me. My partner took it with him before we closed for the night." He doubted if this would be enough to make the robber go away. Worst case scenario, the man would force him back into the bar, and William could show him that the registers were empty.

"Turn around," the man said.

William did so.

By then, the other set of footsteps had stopped, and there were now two goons facing him. Both wore dark clothing and ski masks. Both had guns, but only the taller one was pointing his. William looked from one to the other, hating that they were so prepared. He had a security camera that was recording every moment of this. By concealing their identities, the perpetrators had made it difficult to prosecute them, but what else is new? Blacks committed crimes every day and were rarely prosecuted. Despite their masks, William was certain both of these assholes were black because he could see their skin tone and their big lips through the holes in the masks. Even the short one with fair skin that could pass for white in the darkness was definitely black. Those big watermelon sucking lips were a dead giveaway.

"I don't have any money," he repeated. "My partner, he took it. We never leave money in the bar overnight, and I never have any on me when I close up."

The taller thief said, "William, we're not here for your money. We're here to give you this."

He didn't move to give William anything, but the shorter one did. As the second man raised his hand, William noticed that he was wearing latex gloves, and he'd been holding something the whole time. In one hand was a gun. In the other, as it rose into view, William saw that it was a playing card. The man flipped it over.

It was the ace of spades.

William's eyes flashed wide as the realization of what was happening, what this *really* was, dawned on him. He had only been moderately afraid of these men when they first accosted him. Now terror slapped him hard across the face. His bowels loosened, but he managed to only fart, rather than shit his pants right then and there.

"It's, it's not me," he stammered. "You, you got the wrong person."

"If I had the wrong person, you wouldn't be getting all bent out of shape about this card," Demon reasoned. "I told you I was coming for you."

"*But I didn't mean it*! I was just saying that stuff. *I didn't mean none of it!*"

"You said you weren't scared of '*no niggers*,' you would never let a *nigger* stop you from hating *niggers*, and you couldn't wait for a *nigger* to try to rob you one day so you could kill *another nigger*."

"I didn't mean it. I never did anything. *I never hurt anybody!*"

"You killed Jeremy Nettles."

"*That was self-defense!*"

"That's not what you said on that message board. You said he'd been panhandling in front of your bar, pissing off your customers, and when you closed for the night, he followed you around back, to this area right here, still begging for money. You said he got too close, and you felt it was a good time to kill a nigger. You should've been convicted. If you had that camera installed at the time–" Demon gestured towards the lens that was pointed at them, the one Einstein had already disabled "– you probably *would've* got convicted. But without the camera, the jury bought your story about being in fear for your life. It was late at night, and the guy followed you all the way to your car, demanding money. *Attempted robbery by threat* is the way your defense lawyer put it."

William swallowed roughly. His mouth hung open. He began to shake his head. "It was, it *was* like that. I was scared. He tried to rob me."

"Nah," Demon said. "I think what you saying on those message boards is the real truth."

"It's not. *I swear it's not!*"

"Then why you always on those websites?" Demon wondered. "Out of all the things the world wide web has to offer, why do you spend most of your time on sites that hate niggas, talking about how much you hate niggas?"

"And how come you don't let blacks come to your bar?" Zahra chimed in. "You scare 'em off with the confederate flag you got draped on the wall, or do you tell them flat out that they ain't welcome here?"

207

William felt like his head might explode from an information overload, and not just because the shorter man was actually a woman. These people knew everything about him, which meant the group that called themselves the *Ace of Spades* was real, which meant they planned to gun him down right there in the parking lot and leave the playing card on his corpse, like they'd done in New York, Chicago, Illinois, Iowa, Florida, and a few other places he couldn't think of at the moment.

Knowing he couldn't talk his way out of this, his last coherent thought was of Doc Holliday, the famed gambler, gunfighter, and friend of Wyatt Earp.

I'm your huckleberry.

As legend had it, Holliday was so quick on the draw, he could pull his weapon and gun down two men, even if one of them already had a pistol pointed at him.

His teeth chattering, William took a deep breath and tried his luck.

The last thing he heard was the sound of thunder.

Demon's eyes were as cold as steel as he shot the downed man once more in the face. Zahra tossed the playing card onto the growing pool of blood before she and her man turned and disappeared into the night.

KEITH THOMAS WALKER

ABOUT THE AUTHOR

Keith Thomas Walker, known as the Master of Romantic Suspense and Urban Fiction, is the author of more than two dozen novels, including *Fixin' Tyrone*, *Life After*, *The Realest Ever*, the *Backslide* series, the *Brick House* series, the *Finley High* series and the *Asha and Boom* series. Keith's books transcend all genres. He has published romance, urban fiction, mystery/thriller, teen/young adult, Christian, poetry and erotica. Originally from Fort Worth, he is a graduate of Texas Wesleyan University. Keith has won numerous awards in the categories of "Best Male Author," "Best Romance," "Best Urban Fiction," "Best Young Adult Romance," "Best Duo," "Book of the Year," and "Author of the Year," from several book clubs and organizations. Visit him at www.keithwalkerbooks.com.

9 781735 615134